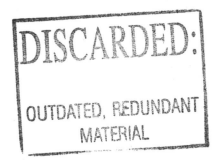

Praise for Beth Vrabel and Pack of Dorks:

"Debut author Vrabel takes three knotty, seemingly disparate problems—bullying, the plight of wolves and coping with disability—and with tact and grace knits them into an engrossing whole of despair and redemption. . . . Useful tips for dealing with bullying are neatly incorporated into the tale but with a refreshing lack of didacticism. Lucy's perfectly feisty narration, emotionally resonant situations and the importance of the topic all elevate this effort well above the pack."

—*Kirkus Reviews,* starred review

"Lucy's growth and smart, funny observations entertain and empower in Vrabel's debut, a story about the benefits of embracing one's true self and treating others with respect."

—*Publishers Weekly*

"Vrabel displays a canny understanding of middle-school vulnerability."

—*Booklist*

"Lucy's confident first-person narration keeps pages turning as she transitions from totally popular to complete dorkdom in the space of one quick kiss. . . . Humorous and honest."

—*VOYA*

"This book doesn't soft-peddle the strange cruelty that kids inflict on one another, nor does it underestimate the impact. At the same time, it does not wallow unnecessarily. . . . The challenging subject matter is handled in a gentle, age-appropriate way with humor and genuine affection."

—*School Library Journal*

"*Pack of Dorks* nails the pitfalls of popularity and celebrates the quirks in all of us! An empowering tale of true friendships, family ties, and social challenges, you won't want to stop reading about Lucy and her pack . . . a heartwarming story to which everyone can relate."

—Elizabeth Atkinson, author of *I, Emma Freke*

"A book about all kinds of differences, with all kinds of heart."

—Kristen Chandler, author of *Wolves, Boys, and Other Things That Might Kill Me* and *Girls Don't Fly*

"Beth Vrabel's humorous debut, *Pack of Dorks*, takes a fresh look at what it means to embrace what makes you and the ones you love different. . . . The novel is a must read for anyone trying to survive fourth grade or anyone who remembers what it was like. *Pack of Dorks* is the pack I want to join."

—Amanda Flower, author of Agatha Award nominee *Andi Unexpected*

"Beth Vrabel's stellar writing captivates readers from the start as she weaves a powerful story of friendship and hardship. Vrabel's debut novel speaks to those struggling for acceptance and inspires them to look within themselves for the strength and courage to battle real-life issues."

—Buffy Andrews, author of *The Lion Awakens* and *Freaky Frank*

"Beth Vrabel weaves an authentic, emotional journey that makes her a standout among debut authors."

—Kerry O'Malley Cerra, author of *Just a Drop of Water*

A BLIND GUIDE TO STINKVILLE

Also by Beth Vrabel

Pack of Dorks

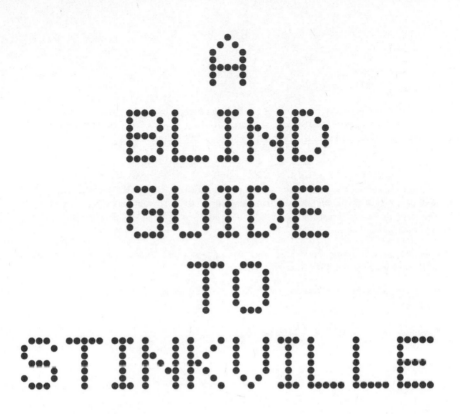

A BLIND GUIDE TO STINKVILLE

BETH VRABEL

Sky Pony Press
New York

Sky Pony Press books may be purchased in bulk at special discounts for sales promotion, corporate gifts, fund-raising, or educational purposes. Special editions can also be created to specifications. For details, contact the Special Sales Department, Sky Pony Press, 307 West 36th Street, 11th Floor, New York, NY 10018 or info@ skyhorsepublishing.com.

This is a work of fiction. Names, characters, places, and incidents are either the products of the author's imagination or used fictitiously.

Sky Pony® is a registered trademark of Skyhorse Publishing, Inc.®, a Delaware corporation.

Visit our website at www.skyponypress.com.

10 9 8 7 6 5 4 3 2 1

Library of Congress Cataloging-in-Publication Data

Vrabel, Beth.
  A blind guide to Stinkville / Beth Vrabel.
    pages cm
  Summary: Leaving her best friend and the familiarity of Seattle for the paper mill town of "Stinkville," South Carolina, twelve-year-old Alice, who lives with albinism and blindness, takes on the additional challenge of entering the Stinkville Success Stories essay contest.
  ISBN 978-1-63450-157-6 (hardback)
  [1. Albinos and albinism--Fiction. 2. Blind--Fiction. 3. People with disabilities--Fiction. 4. Self-reliance--Fiction. 5. Moving, Household--Fiction. 6. City and town life--South Carolina--Fiction. 7. South Carolina--Fiction.] I. Title.
  PZ7.V9838Bl 2015
  [Fic]--dc23

                              2015011256

Cover design by Laura Klynstra
Cover image credit Shutterstock

Print ISBN: 978-1-63450-157-6
Ebook ISBN: 978-1-63450-917-6

Printed in the United States of America

A BLIND GUIDE TO STINKVILLE

To my family. And Chuck.

Chapter One

Even I *could* see that Tooter was no Seeing Eye dog.

The ancient Shih Tzu was about the size of a loaf of bread. His bottom teeth poked out of his mouth all the time. His eyes were once brown but now they were sort of gray. Tooter's favorite thing in the world to do was to rub his butt against the ground. Or the table. Or someone's leg. And to fart. And that's the story behind the name Tooter.

After Mom finally agreed that my brother, James, could walk me to the library instead of making me spend another summer day alone at home (I mean, I guess, technically, it's home, even though it doesn't feel like it yet), he grabbed Tooter's leash from a hook by the door.

"Come on, Alice. Might as well take care of two needy pains-in-the-butt," he muttered.

We moved to Sinkville, South Carolina, about three months ago. Sinkville is the official name, but everyone calls it *Stink*ville.

1

Home, I mean *real* home, is Seattle, Washington. We lived there, right along the shore, all twelve years of my life. There was always a wonderful blanket of soft gray in the sky, so I only had to put on sunscreen once in the morning and my milk-white skin stayed perfectly pale. The air smelled salty and like rain. Mom would walk me to school during the school year, and I'd spend the summer hanging out with my best friend, Eliza, who lived a block from us. Her mom let her walk over to our house by herself in the morning, but of course it was impossible for me to head out on my own. So we'd always hang out at my home. Mom would bake us cookies and tell us stories about her life B.A. (before Alice), when she was a travel writer. She made every day feel like an adventure. Sometimes when Dad came home from work, he'd say, "Where'd ya go today, Alice?" And I'd say anything from Argentina to Zaire, wherever Mom had talked about that day.

Here in Stinkville, life is pretty much the opposite of before. We live in a little house in the middle of the woods. Even with all the trees, the sky is blazing blue. I have to put on sunscreen every other hour. For real. And the air in Stinkville? It smells like rotting eggs. That's because the whole town is centered on M. H. Bartel Paper Mill, where almost everyone (including the new plant manager, a.k.a. my dad) in town works.

2

Do you know how paper is made? I don't either. But I do know it involves purposefully rotting wood. Rotting wood emits incredibly horrible smells. The scariest part: no one in town even smells it anymore. For real. So if we live in Stinkville long enough we'll get used to the stink and we won't even know how horrible it is to new people!

And if that wasn't stinktastic enough, Mom doesn't walk me to school or anywhere for that matter. Mostly that's because we moved in the summer, so there *is* no school. But also because the longer we live here, the less Mom does anything Momish. She took me to the library the first week we were here but has been "too tired," "feeling a little overwhelmed," or "grrrmmlll" (the approximate sound she makes when I nudge her awake), since. She doesn't even tell me to brush my teeth anymore, let alone explain what happened when she went diamond mining in Tanzania years ago.

But what about hanging out all day with my BFF? Well, she's literally across the country. And I'm here. With no friends. No life. My only excitement now is going to M. H. Bartel Public Library (yup, even the library was named after the paper mill).

When James, Tooter, and I got to the library doors, I stomped and refused to go inside without my brother.

"What is your deal?" he hissed. "I said I'd take you to the library, not hold your books for you."

3

"I can't go by myself." I stomped again.

"Why not?"

I glared at him.

"Are you playing the blind card?" he sighed.

"I'm not playing," I snapped. "I'm actually blind. And you have to help me."

"I don't have to do anything," James snapped back. But he looked around for someplace to tie Tooter's leash.

"Do you think it's okay to leave him out here?" I muttered. I mean, it was about a thousand degrees out. Under my enormo sunhat, my sweaty hair felt wet, as if I had just left the shower. Tooter's little pink tongue hung out of his mouth and almost touched the sidewalk.

"Urgh!" James jerked open the door to the library and stepped in, dragging Tooter along by the leash.

The cool fresh air hit my face as we walked inside and I breathed as deeply as I could. My glasses turn to sunglass lenses when I'm outside, so for a minute I was even more blind than usual while the lenses adjusted.

"Excuse me!" a high-pitched voice that seemed to come out of the speaker's nose rather than her mouth called out. "We do not allow animals in here. This. Is. A. Library!"

As my lenses transitioned, I could make out a huge desk in front of us. Behind it, I saw a bright red blur that I think was the speaker's shirt and a fluffy mound of yellow, which had to be her hair.

"I'm sorry," James said. "It's just, I'm bringing my sister here. I had to actually bring her in because she's blind . . ."

"Oh!" The librarian sucked in her breath. I went ahead and rolled my eyes, figuring the person behind the desk was a) Not looking at me, and b) Not able to see behind my dark lenses anyway.

Where we used to live, everyone knew I was blind. It wasn't a big deal. It was accepted, the same way everyone accepted that Josh's mom always was last to pick him up from playdates and that Eliza's hair was too curly to lie flat around her face.

But here, being blind is news. And this is the way it goes when people find out about me: they gasp. Then, if I'm close enough, I'll see this awful expression on their faces, like they just ate some bad cheese but are holding it in their mouths instead of spitting it out. Then they become overly helpful, usually asking the person I'm with what they can do to help instead of asking me. They also speak super loudly, like maybe I'm also deaf. No one ever asks *me* questions.

If they did, I'd be able to explain.

So you've heard of 20/20 vision being normal? I'm 20/200 in my left eye, 20/210 in my right. So a "normal" person could read something from two hundred feet away that I'd have to be twenty feet from in order to read. I know, I know. You're making the bad cheese face for me. Please stop. The point is: I can read. I just have to be really close.

Soon after making the gaspy voice, the librarian came out from behind the desk. My lenses were clearing up. She stood way too close to me, so I could make out that her lipstick was gloppy and pink, and that her yellow hair was gray at the roots. She smelled like lavender mixed with a little rotting eggs. I wonder if that was the paper mill stink on her.

"I am Mrs. Dexter," the librarian said, slowly and loudly.

James snickered beside me, quickly turning it into a cough.

"I'm Alice," I answered.

She stared hard at my eyes, which made me nervous. And that, in turn, made my eyes move faster. So I guess I should just go ahead and say it. I'm blind because I have albinism. You know, like an albino. It just means my skin is about the color of paper, my hair is, too, and my eyes are blue. Everyone who has albinism is visually impaired. We have something called nystagmus, which makes our eyes always move back and forth. A lot of albinos aren't blind like me, though; they are just visually impaired.

"Service animals are welcome in the M. H. Bartel Library, as are any individuals with special needs. Welcome, Alice." Mrs. Dexter said all of this with long. Pauses. Between. Each. Word. "Welcome," she said again.

James now openly grinned at me. He handed me Tooter's leash. The dumb dog was scooting his butt along the carpet but seemed a little peppier in the air-conditioned building.

"Text me when you're ready for me to pick you up," James said. The traitor turned to leave.

"Wait!" Mrs. Dexter stole my line. "Does the Seeing Eye dog know where the large print section is or do I need to tell it?"

"Oh, he'll figure it out," James answered, and all three of us looked down at Tooter, who took the opportunity to sniff his own butt with one stubby leg in the air. "Just let Tooter dig right in."

"Well, Tooter," Mrs. Dexter patted Tooter's head. "Let me know if you need anything."

"Where's the children's section?" I asked.

Mrs. Dexter seemed surprised that I spoke. "It's to the left." Tooter glanced up at her, so she pointed in that direction. "But we don't have Braille children's books here . . ."

"Actually, I can read," I said, walking purposefully to the left. "I just need to get closer." And I think it all would've made a good impression on Bad Cheese Face Librarian had I not tripped.

Ah! The children's section. I stopped at the entranceway and breathed in the smell of books and chaos. From the back of the vast room, I heard giggles and chattering as a preschool program let out. Beside me to the right, tables were set up. And all in front of me, rows and rows and rows of books. Someday I'm going to have a library in my own house. I think I could go ahead and skip the living room and just put in a reading room, with piles of books where the television should be.

Tooter pushed ahead of me and jumped onto a chair that was shaped like an open hand. I scooped him up and sat down in his place, holding him to my lap. The chair was pretty cool but it felt a little strange to be leaning back on a thumb. I reached out, grabbed a book at random, and opened it. I think I would've read the dictionary at that point; I was just so happy to be someplace comfortable. And, just so you know, I can read regular books. I just have to hold the book a couple inches from my face and hope there aren't italics. Nystagmus makes a mess of italics. I use a magnifier to help me read, too.

It's small and sort of looks like a credit card, so I simply keep it in my back pocket.

"Um, you're not actually allowed to bring pets in here." I glanced over the cover of the book, which ended up being *Because of Winn-Dixie*, in the direction of the voice. "That's the rule, even if you are reading a dog book."

In front of me was a girl about my age, maybe eleven or twelve. Her arms were crossed and her voice was super quiet, maybe because we were in a library, but mostly she seemed like the type to always have a quiet voice.

She leaned forward to rub Tooter's fluff-ball head. The girl's dark brown skin made my milky white skin look even more like Oreo stuffing. Tooter tilted his head into her hand and let his tongue roll out of his open mouth. "Kate DiCamillo, the author of your book, writes that it's hard not to fall in love with a dog with a great sense of humor," she said with a slight laugh.

"He's my Seeing Eye dog," I said.

The girl laughed. "Sure he is."

I smiled back. "The lady up front fell for it. So now Tooter is here . . ."

"Mrs. Dexter isn't all there, you know what I mean?" The girl twirled her finger next to her ear and then sat in the other hand chair next to mine. "I'm Kerica, by the way. My mom's the children's librarian. She's going to freak when she sees your dog in here. I want a dog so bad, but she keeps saying no."

"I'm Alice. I just moved here a few weeks ago."

"I figured," Kerica said. "It's a small town. Someone new sticks out."

"They stand out even more if they're an albino."

Kerica snorted. Then she bit her lip and smashed her lips together so hard that I snorted, too. "I'm sorry!" she gasped. "I didn't mean to laugh. But it was just so—"

"Obvious?" I laughed. Soon we were both giggling.

In just a few minutes, I learned a lot of things. First, Kerica spends every summer day, all day, in the library with her mom. She's read about forty books already and it was only the end of June!

"Most of them are dog books," she said, and shrugged in a sad sort of way, which I immediately got. Everyone knows dog stories are a downer. "When I'm tired of reading, I draw pictures of the characters." She flipped open the notebook she was holding and held it up for just a second. I pretended I could see the drawing.

Second, Kerica asks direct questions but they don't feel rude. Like when she asked me if everyone in my family has albinism (nope, just me) and then said, "That must feel a little lonely." That could've made me feel sad, but it didn't. It made me feel like she understood.

"Is that a dog in my library?" a booming voice called out.

Kerica kept on rubbing Tooter's head, who had abandoned my lap for hers the second Kerica had sat down. "Simmer down, Ma. It's a Seeing Eye dog."

Kerica's mom stood in front of me, her arms crossed. She looked so much like a bigger, softer version of Kerica that I had to smile. She watched the two of us for a long moment. "Does Mrs. Dexter know about this animal in here?"

I nodded. "If it helps, I really am blind."

"She's got albinism, Ma."

"'S'at right?" She muttered in the slow southern twang I was still getting used to hearing. She seemed a little caught off guard, but didn't have the bad cheese face.

It's kind of funny. When I lived in Seattle, everyone I knew had always known me. Like Eliza and I had been in the same playgroup when we were babies. Our neighbors had never moved. My elementary school teachers had all taught James before me. Everyone knew everything about me without my ever having to tell them. So I had never had to explain albinism, blindness, or nystagmus to anyone before. They already knew.

But here I was in this library for less than an hour, and I already had to tell three people I was blind. This third time it just sort of slipped out.

"Ma, this is Alice. She's new to town," Kerica said.

"Welcome, Alice. I'm Mrs. Morris. Make sure your dog doesn't do-do in the library." Mrs. Morris started to walk away, then turned back suddenly and rubbed Tooter's head. This was seriously the dog's best day ever.

Honestly, it was *my* best day ever in Stinkville, too.

Chapter Two

T*ooter and* I went to the library every day for the next two weeks. In fact, I was pretty sure we'd be at the library every day forever, so long as I could get James to walk me there. I even packed a lunch for each day (fluffernutter sandwich, string cheese, and an apple that I never ate, but I felt obligated to include something from that food group). I also shoved a bottle of sunscreen in the bag after James guilted me into it.

"*I* got sunburned yesterday," he said. And he was right. His nose was a bright pink color. He and Mom have brownish skin, like they have permanent tans. They both have thick, wavy black hair. Mom's falls to the middle of her waist and is smooth as water when she washes and dries it. Lately it's been in a heavy ponytail or a wild nest around her head, though. James's hair is all over the place, growing down over his forehead and ears and curling up around his neck.

I put my floppy sunhat on my head and coated my arms in sunscreen. Mom kept both stocked in a basket beside the door, so I had no excuses to forget either. Even though we left about nine o'clock in the morning, it was still early enough for my arms to pink up by the time we finished the fifteen-minute walk to the library.

When we woke Mom up that morning, James had told her that he was going to play basketball at the park with some guys. This was news to me since I hadn't seen him with anyone since we moved here. In Seattle, he always had hordes of friends around. But Mom just nodded and said to be sure to drink a lot of water.

It's like she's sort of there lately, once in a while saying Momish things, like, "stay hydrated" and "wear a hat." The next day, she might look surprised to see that you're there, sitting in the living room. Dad says she just needs time to adjust and that we should give her space. Dad certainly is giving her space. He says all the friends we had in Seattle kept her busy and happy. But he's too busy to be around a lot lately. He's gone to the Mill by the time I wake up in the morning and he's back just before—or after—Mom has dinner on the table.

Mom might not be doing her usual what-are-you-*really*-up-to stuff with James and just taking him at his word that he's playing basketball at the park, but when we passed the park on the way to the library I noticed there weren't any guys there. James didn't even have a basketball with him. Instead, he had his skateboard! And now that he had dropped me off at the library, he was heading in the opposite direction from the park.

So far, I've seen two things total in Stinkville: the library and the park. And I've only seen the park because we pass it on the way to the library.

"Where are you going?" I called to him.

"To the lake." James didn't even turn around.

"There's a lake?"

He ignored me, so I shouted, "What kind of lake?"

"The kind with water." Then he threw his skateboard down so it bounced once before he jumped on and wheeled away.

Tooter growled at him and leaned his stubby body against my leg. The dog had never growled at James before. Apparently he was suspicious, too.

"You can't swim!" I shouted in one last attempt to get him to come back.

Two teens walking into the library laughed loudly at that. James was too far away for me to see, but I was pretty sure his ears were red. That's always what happens when I embarrass him. But it was true! He can't swim. He hates getting his ears wet.

"Don't drown!" I added.

I couldn't quite make it out, but I'm pretty sure he flashed a finger he's not supposed to at me.

Tooter tugged at the leash, then raised a leg and peed on the M. H. Bartel Public Library sign. The males in my life are obnoxious.

Rain clouds gathered as I waited for James outside the library that afternoon. They were big enough to spot, gray against white. Even more than that, though, I could smell them. Stinkville gets even stinkier on rainy days. All those clouds act like a tarp to keep the rotting egg smell pushing down on us.

I kept glaring toward the supposed lake for James to appear, but so far nothing. The air was so warm and wet my skin was already damp. Tooter lay on his side on the sidewalk.

"Don't give up," I said to him. "James is just a little late."

Tooter turned around so he was facing the bench where I sat. He bounced twice, getting ready to jump up. When he finally tried the jump, he ended up ramming the edge of the bench with his shoulder, fell back down, turned in a circle a couple times, and lay down.

I had texted James fifteen minutes earlier that I was ready to go and so far nothing. No response.

I chewed on my lip and tried to ignore the *thump, thump, thump* in my chest. My stupid heart was jumping to conclusions. There was a perfectly good reason James didn't respond and hadn't shown up.

Like maybe his cell phone battery had died and he didn't know it yet.

Maybe he got distracted by something but was on his way now.

Or maybe he was lying at the bottom of a lake, drowned.

A distraction! That's what I needed. I thought instead about Sandi Williams. The beautiful, tan blonde girl had been sitting with Kerica on a hand chair when I arrived at the library that morning. The girl was chattering on and on to Kerica, who stared hard at the book in her hands, holding it up over her face the way I have to in order to read. But I knew Kerica didn't need to, so I wasn't sure what was going on. I didn't want to interrupt them, but I didn't know what to do with myself, either.

"So, my mom brought back this gorgeous scarf—Hermes—from Paris. It's silk. She's in Germany right now, but she'll be back by the weekend. We're going to go into the city for sushi and she'll tell me all about what she did. I'm sure it involved some shopping. I don't know what Germany is famous for, but I'm sure I'll get some of it soon. That's just the way *my* mom is, you know. We both get our *space*. We're not on top of each other all the time, like *some* families." There was a slight pause, during which I swear I heard Kerica sigh softly. She definitely turned the pages of her book with way more force than necessary.

Then the girl continued, "Not that there's anything *wrong* with how you're here with your mom right over there all the time, but there is no way that would work for us. But sometime soon Mom is going to take me along on one of her trips. Maybe to Norway next month or . . ."

I guess Tooter had enough of her prattling, or maybe he was mad about not getting space on the chair, because this time he tugged forward on the leash so he was at the girl's feet. Then he growled long and hard. I had never heard him do anything like that before. Fart on a stranger? Certainly. Growl? Never.

"I'm so sorry," I blubbered, pulling back on the leash. But Tooter, though small, is freakishly strong. He dug in his heels and wouldn't move.

"Do you know that you're not allowed to have dogs here?" the girl said. She crossed her arms and tilted her head toward me. All the gushiness of her voice when she spoke with Kerica was gone. Now it sounded burn-you-with-ice frosty.

Tooter tilted his head right back at her, giving the girl the stink eye. I could picture it: the whites of his eyes showing around the colored part.

"Especially vicious dogs," she added.

Tooter turned and pranced over to Kerica, landing in her lap with one leap. He turned around once then sunk down with his head resting on the top of the chair's thumb. He gave the girl the sideways eye again and growled super softly.

"As it happens," said Kerica in a super crisp voice, "Tooter is welcome at the library. He's Alice's service animal."

"Who is Alice?" the girl gasped.

"Um. Me." I stepped forward awkwardly. "I'm Alice."

Kerica jerked her hand toward the girl. "Alice, this is Sandi. She takes classes with my mom a couple times a week. Sandi, Alice."

The girl turned toward me, her eyes raking me from my sunhat, my still dark glasses, my white blonde hair, and my pale skin. I was close enough to notice that her cheeks had flushed when Kerica mentioned she took classes with Mrs. Morris.

"Tooter is a Seeing Eye dog," Kerica said. Tooter farted.

"But she's not blind. She just looked at me and smiled," Sandi said.

"Yes, she is," Kerica snapped.

I just stood there, like a statue.

Sandi actually stood up and moved closer to me. Since I was still holding the end of Tooter's leash, and

Tooter was curled up on Kerica's lap, I wasn't able to move. She was so close I could smell her minty breath.

"How many fingers am I holding up?" she asked.

"It's a trick question," I finally mumbled. "You're not holding any fingers up."

"Ha!" Sandi squealed.

Kerica sighed again. "She has albinism and is *technically* blind. But that doesn't mean she doesn't see *anything*."

"Albinism?" Sandi frowned, her cute little nose wrinkling while she studied me again. "Like an albino?"

I nodded.

"I believe most people with albinism dislike that term." Kerica flipped the pages of her book loudly, not looking at us. She bit off each word with a snap.

"I've never actually seen one of you before," said Sandi, still standing too close for comfort.

"Well, we don't normally come out in the daylight. Usually we only leave our caves at night," I spat out.

Kerica snorted, then all-out laughed, which made me giggle, too.

Sandi didn't move. She just kept staring.

"That was a joke," I finally said.

Sandi didn't twitch but kept staring at me. My glasses had transitioned to clear by then, so I really had nothing to do but stare right back.

"Shouldn't your eyes be pink? I mean, I thought albinos had pink eyes," she said.

"Nope, that's just rabbits. People with albinism have blue eyes, like mine." Sandi squinted into my eyes and I prepped myself for question number two.

"Why are your eyes . . . ? Are you . . . ?"

"It's called stagamus," Kerica said in a duh-everyone-knows-that tone. She lay her head back on a chair finger like our conversation was so completely boring.

"It's, um, nystagmus. Another thing all people with albinism have. It means my eyes move back and forth all of the time," I said.

"How can you see?" Sandi finally spit out.

Kerica shifted in her seat. Tooter farted in response. "Like I said already, being blind doesn't mean she can't see *anything*," Kerica said in the same can't-believe-I-have-to-explain-this tone. She stood up, holding Tooter like a football under her arm, and put her other hand on my shoulder. "She can see stuff, she just has to get closer. It's not a big deal."

I felt the corners of my mouth pop up.

"Want to go sit in the back?" Kerica asked.

I nodded and was about to turn to go when Sandi grabbed my elbows, locking me in place. She stared at me and her eyes narrowed, like she was reading my face. I got the feeling she didn't like my storyline.

I guess it didn't help that Sandi was exactly how you'd expect a South Carolina girl to look, down to the blonde ponytail. She had wide brown eyes, tan skin, and freckles on her nose. I usually can't make out this much detail on people when I meet them. But Sandi was standing about two inches from my face. Her head twitched back and forth while she tried to follow my eyes. It was making me twitchy, too.

"Your eyes! They just got faster!" Her head was practically vibrating now, watching my eyes.

James says my eyes are mood detectors—when I'm nervous, excited, or scared, my eyes flutter. When I'm happy, they're slow and steady as windshield wipers on the lowest setting. Right now: full-on twitchiness.

The squeals and chatter of preschoolers rang out from the back of the library as story time ended. Mrs. Morris's booming voice echoed down the rows of books. "Bye, jellybeans!" she called out. "See you next week!"

Sandi finally turned from me, grabbed her backpack from beside the other chair hand, and thrust it up her shoulder. She turned back toward me, like she was about to ask another question, but at that moment Tooter growled and Mrs. Morris called her to the back classroom.

"See you later," Sandi said. "Oh! I mean—"

"*Good-bye*, Sandi," Kerica sighed.

Thumpity, thumpity, thumpity.

Distraction over, day replayed, I was right back to panic mode. Now my heart was convinced James had died, and it thrashed around like, well, like a drowning person. Why wasn't he here?

I got out my phone and pressed my speed dial button for James. It rang and rang. No answer. I immediately called it again. When I got to voice mail, I did it again. And then again.

"Everything okay?" Kerica asked. I hadn't even heard the doors to the library open behind me. Mrs. Morris had her back to us, locking the doors shut. Their van was the only car in the parking lot. Everyone else had left. Soon I'd be alone. *Thumpity, thumpity, thumpity.*

"I—I just can't reach my brother. He's supposed to pick me up." My voice was as rattled as my heart.

"All right," Mrs. Morris said, "let's give your mama a call. What's your number?" Even though I was holding my own phone, I let Mrs. Morris dial my home number on her phone. I heard it ring and ring. No answer.

"Hmm," Mrs. Morris said. She let the two heavy canvas bags on her shoulders slump down to the sidewalk. "Well, what's your address?" she asked. "I can drop you off."

"Um." I glanced toward the lake again, hoping I'd see the shadow of James rushing forward. "It's Six Locust Lane."

"Locust Lane," Mrs. Morris repeated. "I'm not sure . . . is that off Winchester?"

"I don't know," I whispered.

"Or do you go down Oleander?"

"I don't know!" I hadn't meant to yell. But I had no idea. I just follow James everywhere. I didn't know how to get home. I didn't know how to get ahold of James. I didn't know anything! I didn't know!

"I don't know," I said again, more softly this time.

"Then we'll figure it out," Kerica said. She slipped her hand into mine.

We stood there while Mrs. Morris searched my address on her phone's GPS app and my heart thumped so fast I couldn't feel the break between beats.

"Does your brother ride a skateboard?" Kerica asked. "Is that him?"

She pointed down the sidewalk in the direction of the supposed lake. I was too upset to see anything, even the blur of James rolling toward us, but I nodded anyway. I wasn't sure my knees would hold me up.

James skidded to a stop in front of me.

I flew into him, knocking him off the skateboard and sending us both stumbling back. "You were dead!

You drowned!" My arms wrapped around him and I squeezed, even with Tooter whining in protest at being yanked around.

"Not me. My phone." James pulled my arms off him and took his cell out of his pocket, the screen black. "Battery died. Sorry."

"Sorry? You're *sorry*!" This time I punched him in the shoulder. "I was stuck here waiting for you, thinking you were dead at the bottom of the lake. A lake I didn't even know *existed* until this morning. I couldn't go home myself because I don't know the way. I couldn't get Mom to get me because she won't answer the phone. I couldn't go after you because I have no idea where you go all day! Don't you understand?"

"Chill!" James said. He glanced over at Mrs. Morris and Kerica. "I was just a little late."

"A little late!" I screamed.

"Everything okay now?" Mrs. Morris asked.

I guess it was a valid question, considering I still was pummeling James between sobs.

Chapter Three

James *didn't* talk to me the whole way home yesterday. He didn't even glance over at me when Mrs. Morris laid into us both about responsibility and the importance of knowing how to get from Point A to Point B (I'm guessing Point A was home and Point B the library). James didn't say a word when Kerica leaned into me and whispered, "See you tomorrow, I hope." Neither of us spoke about how the hot, humid thunderstorm brewing overhead made Stinkville even more putrid. And James still didn't say a word when the first stinking raindrop fell from the sky.

When Stinkville's clouds gave up and puked all over us, he just kept walking.

James opened the door to home dripping and shivering, and I almost expected him to slam it in my face. But he didn't. He stood there in shock.

Because we had opened the door to the smell of spicy beef and the sound of chopping lettuce.

Mom made tacos for dinner.

This was sort of big deal, which I guess shows how totally messed up life in Stinkville was for our family. Because Taco Tuesday should not be a surprise.

"Huh," James muttered softly, then turned down the hall to his bedroom. That door he did slam.

Taco Tuesday is James's favorite meal of the week, not that he said thanks to Mom for preparing it. Once Dad came home and we finally sat down for our fiesta, James crunched four hard taco shells with his fist. Then he dumped a handful of shredded lettuce on top, a pile of shredded chicken and hamburger on top of that, covered all of it with cheese, and then slunk to the table, where he slouched as low as possible and shoveled the concoction into his mouth. Mom and I watched him with our mouths hanging open.

I'll admit, I'm not the neatest eater. Apparently other people think it's "gross" to hold up each piece of food in front of your face, flip it around a couple times in your fingers, and then nibble it before putting the whole bite in your mouth. But seriously. If they had popped what they thought was steak in their mouth and it ended up being a glob of fat, or found that a spoonful of tapioca pudding was actually cottage cheese, they'd be a little more hesitant with their food, too.

Even so, Mom and Dad were always on me to eat neater. To sit up straight. To take human instead of squirrel bites. James used to get on my case about it, too. But lately he seemed to be in all-out annoy-the-crap-out-of-Mom mode. And he wasn't nice to me, either. He still hadn't apologized for abandoning me at the library.

It was odd. All this be-mean-to-Mom-and-Alice business started when we moved, and it's not like Mom or I had anything to do with that. It was all Dad. And James was nice to Dad, even though Dad spent all dinner talking on his cell phone, hand over the receiver when he took bites.

I'm not sure why being a paper mill plant manager makes Dad's phone ring so much. I guess it's because the Mill never closes. Seriously, mill workers are there all the time, round the clock. That's why there's a diner—the Williams Diner—right next door, ready to serve breakfast or a milkshake or both around the clock. Dad's a sucker for the milkshakes. Whenever I get into his car, he unloads an armful of Styrofoam milkshake containers into the trash to make room for us.

He must've just had one before coming home because he definitely didn't seem hungry. All he did was push a few refried beans and sprigs of shredded lettuce around his plate while he talked on his phone.

To make matters worse, we were still using disposable plates and utensils because the moving company had lost our real plates and silverware. Mom kept promising to buy new plates and utensils but hadn't yet. But she did buy us sporks. Lucky us. Have you ever tried to spear a piece of plum with a plastic spork? I don't recommend it.

Tooter seemed to be the only one really excited about the spork situation. He patrolled under the table like a snorting, farting cop, schlepping up whatever fell to the floor on the way to our mouths.

I nibbled on the corner of my taco, holding it horizontally so the guacamole didn't slip out. But it did. It missed the plastic plate and landed with a soft plop on the floor, which Tooter quickly lapped up. And suddenly I was very, very sad.

That guacamole.

My eyes watered. Another drop of guac slid from the taco onto my plate.

I really wanted that guacamole. I wanted it back in the taco. It belonged in the taco. Not on the stupid plastic plate. A stupid plastic plate that didn't even belong in this stupid house in stupid South Carolina. That guacamole belonged in a taco, tucked in securely with a real fork, resting on a real plate, in our real house where we would have real conversations, not hunched-over caveman grunts from James, snippy comments from Mom, and secondhand chatter from Dad.

That guacamole.

The slippery, lumpy green-wasted goodness represented every single thing that was wrong right now. Tooter whimpered at my feet.

Tears spilled over. Then they rushed out. And soon I was going to make that ugly can't-keep-it-in cat-howl noise. I swear, I didn't think about it. I didn't plan it. But somehow my entire flimsy stupid plastic plate flew across the table like a Frisbee, sending bits of taco everywhere.

Tooter flew right after it. I don't think he had ever run so fast.

There was total silence from my family. Grunts and slurping sounds came from Tooter. James had some refried beans smeared across his cheek—maybe from my flying taco. Maybe from eating like a caveman. Mom was midbite, spork held inches from her face. Dad's mouth hung open, phone still pressed against his ear.

I stared back at them for a moment, but I was so sad, so angry, so . . . I don't know . . . that they all looked like blurs in front of me. So I got up and ran. And, of course, I knocked my hip on the edge of the table, sending shredded lettuce into the air. I reached my room and slammed the door before the lettuce could even hit the floor.

When my bedroom door creaked open a few minutes later, I was sure it'd be Mom. But then I heard arguing from the kitchen.

"Maybe if you hung up your phone and tuned in a little bit to what's going on here, we'd know something was wrong before our kitchen turned into a taco salad!" Mom shouted.

"Do you have any idea how stressed out I am? And then I get to come home to a miserable house and pick lettuce out of the heating vent!" Dad screamed back. And just then his phone started ringing.

A pan slammed into the sink. James slowly closed my bedroom door.

"You okay?" he asked.

I flopped over on my bed to face him, not even bothering to wipe away the angry tears wetting my cheek. "Why are you acting so mad at Mom?" I snarled.

"Why'd you freak out on the taco?"

"The guac spilled."

James nodded, like I had reacted in a completely understandable way to slippery guacamole. He sat on the edge of my bed. His shaggy hair hung over his eyes.

"Seriously." I propped myself up on an elbow. "Why are you so mean to her lately?"

Even though James and I looked different in terms of skin and hair color, we've got the same face. So I sort of recognized his expression when he sat down. He was just as lost as me.

"It's her job to stop him, you know?" James's voice was soft, but edgy.

I shook my head. "Nope. I don't know what you mean."

"Think about it, Alice." He leaned back. "It's her job to rein Dad in when he has dumb ideas. And moving here? It was an incredibly *dumb* idea."

"Like when he wanted to sell our house and buy alpacas that one time?"

"Exactly." James's lips quivered like he was trying not to smile. I got that. Sometimes I try to hold on to my anger, too. Dad's usually really good at making someone laugh when they really want to be angry. I gave it a shot.

"Think of all the comfy sweaters we could have had."

James huffed out of his nose, probably the closest thing to a laugh I had heard from him in weeks. "Well, if she's not going to show him that this was a mistake, I will."

Chapter Four

*I*couldn't sleep that night. Mostly because of what James had said, but also because I was starving. That guacamole.

I snuck into the kitchen after everyone had gone to sleep, climbed up on the countertop, and squinted at the green lights on the microwave. It felt like midnight, but it was only ten. Had everyone else gone to bed already? Dad used to stay up until midnight and James until who knew when. I guess they were all exhausted from cleaning up my tacoplosion.

I grabbed a yogurt from the fridge and picked up my magnifier along with the book I had checked out from the library that afternoon. I was trying to catch up with Kerica's book tally, but had so far only finished *Winn-Dixie*. I tried to read but just couldn't stop thinking about what James had said. How was he going to convince Mom and Dad to move back to Seattle?

As I thought about it some more, going back would be so awesome! I knew a different family had moved into our house, but maybe they hated it there as much as we hated it here. Maybe we could swap houses. If James really had a plan and made it work, then I could be hanging out with Eliza by next week. We could spend the day decorating her chalkboard-painted wall. I had helped her and her mom paint a whole wall of her room in the thick black paint last summer. Since then, we decorated it all the time, adding flowers and leaves or continuing our never-ending game of tic-tac-toe. She was going to be so excited when I told her the news! I bet she missed me even more than I missed her. After all, at least I had met Kerica. Eliza was stuck with the same people, the same faces, and I know none of them could replace me.

I put down my library bag and picked up the iPad, plugging in my oversized monitor. In Seattle, it was only 7:00 p.m. I tapped the green app and Eliza picked up on the third Facetime ring.

"Kerica sounds pretty boring."

That's the thing about Eliza, she never holds back how she feels.

"She's nice! You'd like her a lot."

Eliza scrunched up her face, like she seriously doubted it. "Whatever . . ."

36

"Whatever," I mumbled back, not sure why I was even bothering to defend Kerica. It's not like we were best friends or anything. "How's Kenny?" I finally said, changing the subject.

Kenny was the love of Eliza's life. Three years older than us, he had lived next door to Eliza forever and had yet to acknowledge her existence. Here's something you should know about Eliza: she's the yin to my yang, the jelly to my peanut butter, the chocolate to my milk. We're exact opposites, but somehow that works for us. Eliza has curly brown hair cut boy short, wears silvery eye shadow and pink glossy lipstick, never worries about what to say, and makes up her mind in seconds. Years ago, she decided Kenny was the boy she would marry and getting him to realize the inevitability of that became the crux of our fourth-grade year. Me? I think boys are gross. But as Eliza's best friend, I've got to be supportive.

"Kenny?" Eliza made a face that looked like the name itself was like a burst of morning breath. "He's so lame."

"What?" I gasped. "A week ago you were naming your future babies!" Eli and Iza. Seriously. Luckily, I figured I had a few decades to talk Eliza out of those names.

Eliza shrugged. She seemed suddenly very interested in flaking off a bit of her bright blue nail polish. "So, these twins moved into your old house."

"Oh." I knew that a family had moved in to our old house, which was a block from Eliza's. But it felt weird hearing about the new people living there. Someone in my bedroom, hanging stupid posters on my grape-colored walls, probably. "What are they like?"

"They're actually really, really cool." Eliza bounced, making the screen suddenly reflect the glow-in-the-dark stars on her ceiling. Eliza's a bouncer; whenever she's really into whatever she's talking about, she literally can't sit still. "Sam—she's a girl—is a dancer. But not ballerina dancer. Hip-hop. She's shown me some moves, and, man, that girl can dance! And Morgan—he's a boy— he's . . ." Her face flushed.

"He's the new Kenny?"

"Alice!" Eliza flopped back on her bed. "He's amazing. He's tall, he listens to cool music, and he's got perfect teeth. I think he's the one."

I caught myself before my eyes fully rolled. That's a bad habit of mine. It took me a long time to figure out that other people could actually see me roll my eyes at them even if I was across the room. So I stopped mid-roll and pretended I had noticed something on my ceiling. Not that Eliza had even been paying attention. She was still prattling on about Sam this, Morgan that.

"Which one's in my room?" I interrupted her in the middle of telling me how Sam was taking her to a dance class later that week.

"Morgan." Eliza grinned. "You won't believe it. He painted the walls black!"

I bit my lip, hard, trying to dislodge my stupid tears. The water stayed still in my eyes. "Huh," I swallowed, willing my voice to stay steady. "Like your wall, with the chalkboard paint?"

"No, shiny black." Then Eliza was the one to roll her eyes. "Chalkboard paint is so childish, you know. Morgan's giving me his leftover paint to cover it up. It looks incredible," Eliza gushed. "He even painted all the trim around the doors and windows black. Can you believe it? Their parents are so cool to let them paint their rooms like that."

"The trim, too?" I echoed. The trim where Dad had added a notch every year on my birthday to show how much I had grown? He had even scribbled what my special birthday dinner was beside the notch (Age 4: "Spaghetti and angel food cake decorated with gummy worms and Spider-Man"; Age 8: "Mushroom pizza with chocolate lava cupcakes"). Now it was all gone.

From another room, I heard Eliza's mom yell, "Eliza! Sam's here!"

"Oh, gotta go! Bye, Alice!" The screen went black.

I don't know when I finally fell asleep that night, but it had to be close to dawn. Dad once described how the Mill churned pieces of chopped up wood, called pulp, in huge vats, cooking them so all the pieces mushed and stuck together, ready to be flattened and dried out into paper.

My mind was one of those huge vats, taking everything I wanted and everything I dreaded and churning them until they were molded together.

I wanted to go home to Seattle, but it wouldn't be the same if we did. Morgan painted my room black! And even if his family did want to trade with ours (what a childish, stupid idea!), Eliza wouldn't want him to leave. Not now that he was the new Kenny. We'd have to find a new neighborhood in Seattle, and how would that be any different than here? I mean, aside from the horrible stench of Stinkville being replaced with Seattle's salty air. But I'd still have to be Blind Alice instead of just Alice. And maybe Mom would be happier in Seattle again, but what about Dad? Would we see even less of him while he tried to find a new job? And maybe he'd be the sad one then. I thought of Tooter on Kerica's lap,

Mrs. Morris holding a book just for me on the library table, the hand chair waiting for me in the library.

When I finally woke up, the sun was slanting through my bedroom blinds.

James was pouring syrup over a stack of microwavable pancakes when I stumbled into the kitchen. He always drenches them with sticky syrup before nuking them so all the liquid is absorbed.

"I don't think we should move back," I told him.

James's hand stilled over the pancakes, the syrup still rushing out of the bottle. "You're joking, right?"

"No." I sat down on one of the stools. James closed the syrup lid and shoved the pancakes in the microwave, slamming the door shut so hard I thought the plastic would crack.

"What is wrong with you? You hate it here!" he said.

"New people moved into our house. They painted my room black! We'd have to go somewhere new anyway."

"Someplace new in Seattle is better than any place here," he snapped.

"I don't know," I said, realizing I sounded like Dad. "Maybe we just need to adjust."

"You're not seriously buying Dad's crap, are you? Come on, Alice! *You* especially have got to know we're never going to *adjust* to South Carolina."

"What do you mean, *me especially?*"

41

The microwave beeped and James grabbed his plate, slamming the door shut again. He didn't answer me, just shoved forkfuls of pancake into his mouth like he was trying to force himself quiet.

"What do you mean?" I shouted this time.

"Are you really going to make me say it?" he answered finally, in a quiet pancake-less voice.

"Say what?"

"What do you think it's going to be like when school starts, Alice? Do you think you're going to fit in here? Really? I mean, come on, you've got to see . . ."

He let his words fall like bricks around me, echoing louder than any slammed microwave door.

"You don't think I can do it," I whispered. "You don't think I'll be able to fit in here. Or anywhere, really. Is that it?"

James's plastic spork cracked in half in his fist. He glared at me. "Do *you*?" He threw it and the plastic plate in the trashcan. "You know what? Fine. You be happy here. You're just going to have to do it on your own. Have you noticed? Mom's checked out. Well, guess what? So have I. Find your own way to the library today." And with that, James stomped out the front door.

"What's going on in here?" Mom entered the kitchen just as James rushed out the door. She was dressed.

Her hair was pulled back into a ponytail, but I noticed it had been combed. "Alice?" she asked. "What's going on?"

"You've adjusted," I whispered.

"What?"

I rushed into her arms instead of answering her. She squeezed me back, but just for a second. In that moment, I noticed that her fingernails were chewed back to the skin. She smelled like deodorant, but sort of stale, too. Not entirely like Mom. She sort of patted my back and then moved to make coffee.

"What should we do today?" she asked.

"Um, I've been going to the library. We could do that."

"All right. Let's go to the library." Mom's smile was stuck on her face, not quite making it to her eyes.

"We don't have to," I said. "We could just stay home."

Mom shook her head. "Nope. I've been meaning to get to the library, anyway. I want to do a little research."

The farther we walked away from the house, the more I saw Mom wasn't actually that well-adjusted after all. We used to go for these types of walks along the waterline in Seattle. Her hand would be loose in mine, our arms swinging, and she used to describe everything—birds flying by with red wings, clouds that looked like elephants, flowers blooming on apartment balconies. She'd tell me about them in such detail that I could see them, really see them, even though I couldn't, really. Most of the time, I'd squeeze my eyes shut so I could see everything clearer in my mind. But if there was something tiny, like a bug or a caterpillar, we'd stop and study it, Mom holding it on her long, thin fingertips and standing still so I could make out each detail.

Yet on the way to the library today, her hand held mine tight as a belt. Her shoulders were stiff and her eyes were kept staring straight ahead. She didn't point anything out to me like she used to. Just step, step, step.

And now we were there and she still hadn't told me what she was wanting to research at the library. She followed me into the children's section where Kerica was waiting for me in our hand chairs.

"Is that your mom?" Kerica whispered as I sat down.

I nodded.

"She's pretty."

"Yeah, I know," I said.

"She looks like you when you first came here."

"What do you mean?" Mom and I look nothing alike. Kerica shifted in her seat and opened her book. "What do you mean?" I asked again, a little louder.

She shrugged. "A little . . . I don't know. Stiff."

"I don't know what you're talking about." Then I realized how uptight I sounded, so I stretched out like I was made of liquid. Kerica giggled and I grinned back, finally starting to feel less worried.

I was just about to spill everything that had happened onto Kerica's lap—the conversation with Eliza, the fight with James, the weird way Mom had been acting. I knew it would be a little awkward. I mean, Kerica and I had just gotten to know each other. Really, I didn't know anything at all about her yet, other than she reads a lot and she can be really snarky. But it'd be so nice to be able to dump my brain onto someone, the way I used to be able to with Eliza. And I had a feeling she'd give good advice.

"The truth is—"

"Do you two, like, *live* in here?" Sandi sauntered up to us and let her backpack slide down her arm to fall with a thud by her feet. "I mean, it's summer. Summer! I come here because I *have* to, when I should be swimming, shopping, or even sleeping. But you two . . ."

Kerica took three deep, loud breaths through her nose. Then in her snotty only-when-Sandi-is-around voice said, "Why don't you share with us just *why* you *have* to be here, Sandi. I'm sure that'd be interesting."

Sandi's tanned face flushed. She sort of twitched a little. "That's none of your business," she snapped.

Kerica picked up her book and held it directly in front of her face. I had a feeling she was smiling behind it.

"Alice." Mom held a bunch of pamphlets in her hands. She shoved them into her big shoulder bag. "Are you ready to head back?" I bent to pick up one of the pamphlets that she had dropped.

The type on the pamphlet was three times the normal size, so I easily read it even though I wasn't holding it close to my face. "Addison School for the Blind," I read out loud. "Mom?" I guess it came out a little squeaky and loud because suddenly even the hushed voices in the library snuffed out.

Mom's gaze shifted between Kerica, who was now peeking over the top of her book, and Sandi, who grabbed the pamphlet out of my hand. "So, you really are blind? Huh," she semi-snorted.

Mom sighed. "Your dad and I decided the best option for you would be a specialized school, Alice. We're just looking into which one."

"What about me?" I asked. "Don't I get a say?"

"We'll talk about this at home. Let's go." Mom's voice was strained and tired. She turned to leave.

I grabbed her arm and turned her back around. "But I've always gone to public school."

Mom ran her hands along her pulled-back hair, smoothing a few stray pieces in place. "In Seattle,"

Mom snapped, "where we knew everyone. This is going to be different. You're going to need to learn skills, like how to get around and how to use the vision you have—how to live independently."

"You can show me these things! I can learn them myself."

"Home, Alice. Let's go." She turned and began walking away, but I stayed rooted next to the hand chair.

"Why can't you show me?" I shouted at her back.

"Because I don't know how!" she screamed.

Now I heard chairs shift as people turned to watch us. Mrs. Morris paused in the middle of hanging a poster on the bulletin board. "Everything okay?" she asked.

"Yes, we're just leaving," Mom said in a fake pleasant voice. She turned toward me again and took three quick strides so she was so close I could smell her sour coffee breath. Her eyes squeezed shut and her lips were pressed so hard together they looked white. She hissed, "We've made quite enough of a scene here. Let's go."

Mrs. Morris hummed a little as she put flyers in stacks around the room and shooed kids around in their seats as Mom and I glared at each other. Any time she got close to someone, she shoved a flyer at them. "Sinkville Success Stories, read all about it. Essay contest for Sinkville children!"

"Flyer?" Mrs. Morris shoved one into Sandi's hand. "You could go sit down somewhere and read it. Kickstart our tutoring for the day."

"No, thanks," Sandi said. "This is more entertaining."

Mom and I kept right on glaring.

"Sandi," Mrs. Morris said a little too chipper in the background, "this could count toward your summer work. And there's a cash prize. Two hundred dollars!"

Sandi snagged the flyer from her hand but didn't move away from the showdown.

"Flyer?" Mrs. Morris handed one to me, forcing me to lose the glare war. Moms. They're always on the same side. "You could win a contest!"

I held up the flyer. Sinkville Success Stories was printed across the top.

"Thanks, Mom," Kerica said in a high-pitched fake voice as Mrs. Morris shoved a flyer at her, too. "Think I should enter?"

Mom and I resumed glaring.

"Oh, yes," Mrs. Morris said in the same odd high pitch. "You could win a certificate!"

Still glaring.

Mrs. Morris cleared her throat and then read the rest of the flyer aloud: "Our town has been incorporated for more than one hundred and twenty-five years, yet all anyone seems to know about it is the M. H. Bartel Paper

Mill and the smell that comes from the millwork. Share all the ways Sinkville is more than just its smell and you could win two hundred dollars, a trophy, and town recognition. The award-winning town guide will kick off Mayor Marshall's campaign to change our town's reputation!"

Mom and I kept glaring. I was first to crack. Again.

"Maybe," I hissed, "instead of special schools for me, you should look up special places for you. Places that will teach you how to get around and how to fit in. Because I might be blind, but you're the one who doesn't leave the house or get dressed or take care of stuff."

Mom's cheeks turned bright red and her eyes filled. I felt a little sorry, but just like I couldn't stop myself from throwing that taco, I couldn't hold back from slapping her with more words. "You used to want to help me. Now you don't even get out of bed, except on days when you want to ruin my life."

"I'm doing the best I can," Mom's whisper voice cracked. "I'm not . . . I'm not well right now."

Sandi stepped closer, her eyes wide as she listened to our hushed fight. I glanced over at Kerica, who still held the flyer in front of her face. But I knew she was listening, too.

"Then you need to try harder."

Mom grabbed my arm and turned to leave again. "This is not the place, Alice—"

I yanked my arm free and stomped my foot. "But we just got here!" I sat down in the hand chair and smoothed the flyer on my lap. "I need to get started on the contest."

Mom stared at me. I could feel her eyes boring into the top of my head. "Fine," she said after a couple minutes. "I'll pick you up later."

"I'd be happy to take her home this afternoon," Mrs. Morris murmured to Mom. She put her arm around Mom's waist and they walked like that toward the front desk, talking in low voices.

I couldn't sleep again that night. The glowing numbers of my alarm clock flashed ten o'clock. Sighing, I grabbed my iPad and dialed Eliza's number.

"Hey, Alice!" Eliza picked up on the second ring. She looked totally different, with glossy red lips and smooth hair. Well, half her head had smooth hair. Someone stood behind her but I couldn't see the person's face.

"Who is it?" the person—a girl's voice—asked. She grabbed a chunk of Eliza's hair and ran it through a straightener. Eliza's wild curls fell from it like shiny black paper. The girl's face dipped into the screen. I tried not to glare at the way her jaw popped open. "Are you, like, okay?" she said to me. To Eliza, she said, "Is she sick?"

Eliza's cheeks flushed. She laughed. "No, this is Alice. She lived in your house. She's just sort of pale." Ah. So the girl must be Sam, the hip-hop dancer who stole my house and was now after my best friend.

"Who?" Sam said. She stood and grabbed another chunk of Eliza's hair, so all I saw was her hands and chest.

"Alice. I told you about Alice," Eliza said.

"Nah. Don't think you did. But whatever. Hi, Alice," Sam said, half smiling at the screen.

Eliza hadn't even *talked* to her about me? Her best friend since kindergarten? What the heck! I felt my nostrils flare as I took deep breaths.

"Everything okay, Alice?" Eliza asked.

Part of me wanted to hang up, but I really needed to talk to someone. I needed a friend. "Can we talk?" I asked.

Eliza giggled. "We are talking, silly."

Stupid Sam laughed, too.

"Alone, I mean. Can I talk to you alone? For just a minute." Sam dropped Eliza's hair.

"That's kind of rude," Eliza said.

"No, it's cool. Just come over to my house after you're done," Sam told Eliza. "And don't take too long! I want to practice our moves for the party this weekend."

"Party?" I asked once I heard Eliza's bedroom door snap shut.

Eliza crossed her arms. "Yeah. Sam's teaching me a dance for a party she invited me to."

"Oh."

After about thirty seconds of being quiet, Eliza snapped, "Well, what did you want to talk about?"

I gulped. "I miss you. I miss . . . everything."

Eliza dropped her arms. "I miss you too, Alice." She flopped back on the bed, holding the iPad. Finally she looked like my friend again. "So, what's up?"

"My mom and I got in a huge fight. She wants me to go to a school for blind kids. Can you believe it?"

Eliza didn't respond for a while. "But you *are* blind," she finally said.

"I'm not *that* blind, though! I've always gone to public school!"

Eliza's lips twisted like she was chewing her words before she said them. "Do you know that your mom and mine worked it out so that we'd always be in the same class?"

"Yeah," I said.

"I'm glad they did," she said, "don't get me wrong. But it was so that I could make sure you got where you needed to be and had everything you needed."

"So?" I snapped.

"So, we never really tried to make other friends. And, since you've been gone, I've really gotten to know loads of other kids. Not just Sam, but kids we've been in class with forever and never really talked with because it was always just us. I *liked* helping you, but maybe if you could do things on your own, I would've been friends with them all along. I'm kind of . . . popular now. Can you believe it?" She actually grinned at me, like I should cheer or something. She sat up and bounced on the bed.

"Sorry to be such an inconvenience!" I snapped.

"Stop, Alice! I don't mean it like that. I just think, maybe it'd be good for you to figure stuff out on your own. Maybe it wouldn't be such a bad thing. Maybe you could make friends with people more like you."

"I can't believe you just said that," I stormed. My heart hammered and my throat felt too tight.

"Alice, all of this is coming out wrong! I just mean—"

"Whatever, Eliza. You better go. Sam—and all of your other friends—are waiting for you. I don't want to hold you back."

Dad woke me up the next morning. "Come on, sweetheart," he said, "let's get some breakfast."

"Shouldn't you be at work?" I asked, grabbing at his tie. His breath smelled like coffee. Why did parents drink that stuff? It tasted awful and it didn't smell good, either. But I had cried myself to sleep the night before and breathing in something so familiar—even if it was bad coffee breath—made me feel a little better.

He pulled the tie from my hand and swatted me softly across the nose with the end of it. "First, we're going to breakfast."

I was so excited I forgot my glasses, just pulled on some clothes and rushed out to meet him in the kitchen.

"Go wake up your brother," said Dad, punching out a text on his cell phone and not looking up.

I stopped outside of James's door, not really wanting to face him. When I returned from the library I had wanted to talk to him about the school-for-the-blind pamphlets. But now, I didn't want to face him. Maybe it was babyish, but I just wanted Dad to myself.

I rapped a little with my knuckle and his door swung open. No James.

I skipped back to the kitchen. "He already left!" I sung to Dad.

"Huh," he said, still staring at his phone. "You think he checked in with Mom?"

"Yeah," I said, even though I was pretty sure James left without telling anyone.

"Okay, then," Dad said. "Let's go."

Dad's phone rang four times on the way to Williams Diner, which is just across the street from the Mill. It's sort of the nexus of the stench. I held my T-shirt up over my nose like an oxygen mask. It gave the rotting eggs smell an edge of laundry detergent freshness.

"Stop it," Dad whispered in my ear as we got out of the car. "You're being rude."

"But it's ruining my appetite," I whispered back.

He yanked the shirt down over my nose. "They're watching you." Dad jerked his face toward people walking into the diner. This made my eyes widen. People were watching me? I couldn't make out their faces; the early morning sun was so bright my eyes stung and made even squinting painful. Have you ever gotten a paper cut on your eyeball? Me, neither. But I've got to think it feels a lot like how much my eyes were burning. Except maybe instead of one paper cut, I had a thousand or so. By the time we entered the diner, my face was streaked with tears.

"What's wrong with the lil' miss?" someone asked as Dad led me inside. The man's voice sounded like dried mud. "Gretel!" he called out. "Little kid here's hurt!"

"It's the sun," my dad answered, leading me by the elbow to a table. "I forgot to make her wear a hat.

This happens sometimes when she goes from a dark car to the bright light."

I tried not to whimper, but it still really hurt.

"Will this help?" Between my wet lashes and blurry eyes, I saw a wide, warm hand with bright pink nails. It held a dripping wet cold cloth, which the hand pressed to my eyes. Instant relief! "S'okay, honeybun," the woman said, and suddenly my heart hurt worse than my eyes.

"Grandma?" I asked. I knew it couldn't be; my dad's mom had died two years earlier. But this voice, it had the same tea-with-honey sweetness as hers. My eyes started to sting again, but not from the sun.

The woman chuckled, and she squeezed my hand with hers. All around me, I heard shuffling of feet and questions as people crowded around us.

"She all right?"

"What she need?"

"My daughter's a doctor; let me give her a call!"

"Nah, nah, she's fine," Dad said. He wrapped his arm around my shoulder. "She just is sensitive to the sun."

"Course she is. Looks like a porcelain doll," the woman with Grandma's voice said. "Bet she pinks up faster than an egg fries."

The feet shuffled back to waiting tables. Dad and the woman talked back and forth—ordering breakfast,

I think—but I couldn't concentrate on the words. I just listened to the voices.

After a few minutes, I heard the clink of plates being lowered on the table. I took the damp cloth from my eyes. Dad and I were sitting on the same side of a red vinyl booth. The table had a gray flecked Formica top. On top of it was a plate of the biggest, fluffiest pancakes I had ever seen. They were piled high with cherry sauce and whipped cream.

"Wow!" I murmured.

"Your dad thought you'd like these!" Grandma's voice said. I looked up at the woman. She must've been about sixty, with blonde hair tied back in braids and clipped at the back of her neck. Grandma had had fluffy dark curls and was super thin and tiny. This woman was rounder and younger. Grandma never wore any makeup and her face was always shiny. This woman's face was powdered and matte and her lips were a very unnatural shade of cotton candy pink.

She watched me steadily as I stared at her face. "See, not your grandma after all. My name's Gretel."

Dad squeezed my shoulder again. "Gretel owns the Williams Diner." He slurped on a plastic straw sticking out of a Styrofoam cup, momentarily distracting me.

"Is that a milkshake? For breakfast!" I asked.

Gretel chuckled again. "All he eats is milkshakes!"

"Hey!" Dad put his hands up like he was holding us back. "It's coffee flavored!"

Dad sucked down his milkshake and I tackled the mountain of pancakes. After every few slurps, Dad would point out someone or something in the diner. Like the man who perched at the counter like a bald eagle. He had a newspaper in his hands, but Dad told me the man never read a word. He got all his news listening to the people around him. Dad told me the man, the only one there wearing a suit other than Dad, was Mayor P. Harold Marshall. That's how he introduced himself to newcomers like us, but Dad said everyone called him Hank.

"The only one who calls him Harold is Gretel. Hank's here at opening every morning, leaves for a couple hours, comes back for lunch, and I usually see his pickup in the lot when I head home at dinner." Dad leaned in close and whispered in my ear, "I think he's in love with Gretel."

"Or at least with her milkshakes," I whispered back as Gretel handed the man a Styrofoam cup like Dad's.

When the bell on the door rang out to announce another diner, I turned in my seat. A girl led an elderly man to the booth across from us. It was so close I could touch the booth with my outstretched hand. The girl, who looked about James's age, didn't sit down. She got up to grab a couple place settings and a paper placemat and brought them to the table.

"Morn'n'." The old man nodded toward Dad and me. There was something funny about his grin, which the girl also seemed to notice when she sat down.

"Gramps!" she snapped. "Why didn't you put your teeth in this morning?"

The old man chuckled like not wearing your teeth to a restaurant was the best joke ever. Then he pulled them out of his pocket. He turned and blew on his dentures and I sneezed as a little cloud trickled to my nose.

"I'm so sorry!" the girl exclaimed.

"Ah, just a little sawdust," the old man said. "Never hurt anybody." He dipped his dentures in the cup of water, shook them a little, and slipped them in his mouth.

I giggled and he smiled at me, popping the teeth out and back in to make me laugh harder. Then he reached in his other pocket, blew off sawdust in the other direction, and handed me a little piece of wood covered in smooth ridges. I held it close to my face to check it out and slowly breathed, "Whoa!" I got my magnifier out of my back pocket to check out the details. The little piece of wood, only the size of my thumb, was so intricately carved into a little man with a peaked hat and beard that I had no choice but to smile back at its grin. In its hand, it held a dandelion, with half the wishes blown away. I felt little bumps across the gnome's chest, which I think were little seeds scattered as if they were caught by the breeze.

"It's a gnome," the old man said. His cheeks were a little pink.

"It's amazing," I said. "Did you carve it?"

"All he does is carve," the girl muttered.

Reluctantly, I handed it back to the man.

"Nah." He patted my outstretched hand with his calloused fingers. "You keep him. Gnomes are good luck."

Funny how that little gift made my eyes get watery again. "Thank you," I whispered.

Dad and I finished our breakfast slowly, him watching the people around us and me listening to him whisper descriptions.

"It's not so bad here, is it?" Dad said as the silence between us stretched thin as taffy.

"It's so different," I answered, running my thumb along my gnome's wished-away seeds.

"But the people . . ." Dad tilted his head toward the counter where Gretel was laughing in Grandma's voice. She swung by, putting a milkshake in front of the old man and telling him she added some extra love.

"When you gonna marry me, Gretel?" the old man asked.

"Ha! You know me, married to this diner for the past forty years," she laughed.

Next to us, the teenage girl was gently scolding her grandpa again, this time for drinking his milkshake too quickly. Mayor Hank was shaking hands with a mill worker. The door's bell rang again, bringing with it the sour smell of the Mill and a half-dozen greetings for the newcomer.

I closed my eyes and thought of Mrs. Morris, Kerica, and even Sandi. "The people aren't so bad," I finally said.

"I know it's been tough. I get it. We moved you and your brother, everything is different, and we're making decisions for you that you might not want or like," Dad said, his hand curled around his empty milkshake cup. "But this is where we're at. I need someone—you—to be on my side. Like it or not, this is where we are." Dad nudged me with his elbow. "But it'd be pretty awesome if you liked it."

I smiled, squeezing the gnome in my hand. "I'll try. But Mom and James—"

"I know," Dad said, "they haven't seen the good yet." Dad squeezed his eyes shut and rubbed at them with his thumb and forefinger. "Don't take this the wrong way, Alice, but it's kind of funny to me that you're the one who has started to see the good. You know . . ."

"Because I'm blind?"

Dad smiled, but it was a sad sort of smile. "It's funny to hear you say it like that. Like it's a fact. We've spent so much time trying to make you having albinism and being blind not, I don't know, a factor. Your mom worked so hard to make it not a big deal, not even really a thing. Then we move and suddenly, it's so—"

"Something to deal with," I finished for him. "I know. But I'm not any different than I was in Seattle. I can still do stuff. I'm still me."

"Yeah, but your mom, she's not doing well with the move. She's not there advocating for you. Not because she doesn't care or she doesn't worry. Believe me, she does. But she's struggling." Dad ran his thumb down the side of the cup, the scratching sound breaking the air around us. "You don't know this, but she's been like this before. After James was born, it took a few months. When she realized she could take him with her and still work, it seemed to help. After you were born, she was so blue it took both of us four months to notice that your eyes worked differently."

Dad hung his head lower. "I shouldn't be dumping this on you."

"No." I slipped my hand over his like I was the grown-up. "I want to know."

"I thought it'd make her worse, you know. Finding out you were blind. But it almost kick-started her feeling better. Suddenly she had a mission—to be your advocate. But I'm not sure if she's up to it right now."

"Then I'll do my own advocating," I said with more confidence than I felt.

"It might not be that simple." Dad squeezed my leg. "But I'm proud of you. I'm proud of you for trying."

"I'm not going to that school, though."

Dad shrugged. "Nothing is decided. We're just exploring all the options. We're going to do what's best for you, even if you don't realize it."

"I'm not going."

"We'll see."

Stomach stuffed, I sadly left half my pancakes at the table when Dad said it was time to go. I thanked the old whittler man again as we headed out. Mayor Hank was using thumbtacks to post a flyer by the door. He handed us an extra copy. It was about the Sinkville Success Stories contest.

"Where now?" I asked Dad as we got in the car.

"Home," Dad answered, and it sounded like a heavy word, one that fell between us like a brick. Because, for a few moments in the diner, it did feel like our home was here. Now if only I could get James and Mom to see that. "Home for you, work for me."

"Can we go to Target or Walmart first?" I asked.

"Do you need something?" Dad asked.

"Plates," I answered. "Plates and real forks."

Dad laughed. "Yeah, we can make a pit stop for those."

Chapter Five

Wrestling piglets isn't a usual gig for a journalist, even a journalist whose usual gig is traveling the world. But when Mom was sent to Montana, she wasn't given any instruction other than to find a "slice of life story." That's journalism code for "we have pages to fill." After spending the day hiking and not seeing anything particularly page-worthy, Mom ended up at a rodeo. She made the mistake of telling one of the cowboys that she was a *Geographic World* magazine journalist.

Soon a twangy voice called over the loudspeaker: "We have a real-live reporter visiting us from Geographic World magazine! Would Dana Confrey come down to the rodeo floor?" Not knowing what else to do, Mom made her way down to the dirt ring. The loudspeaker continued, "Miz Confrey's looking for a rodeo story, so we're gonna give her one to remember. She's gonna kick off tonight's rodeo with some pig wrangling."

Before she could say no, Mom was pushed out into the rodeo dirt. From a far corner the gate opened. Out came a squealing greased piglet.

"What did you do?" I had asked Mom when she told me this as a bedtime story years ago.

"What could I do? I wrestled that greasy pig to the ground."

I stood just outside Mom's bedroom door the next morning, wanting to tell her I'd try harder, that I was sorry. But Mom didn't come out. James brushed against my shoulder in the hall.

"Where are you going?" I asked, noticing he already had a backpack on his shoulder.

"The lake."

"It goes by the library," I pointed out.

"I'm leaving now."

I rushed to change out of my pajamas. The only thing I had clean was a pair of too tight jean shorts and a T-shirt. Maybe part of this advocating for myself could be getting Mom to teach me how to do laundry.

Even though I was desperate to leave when James did, I ran back to my room for my cane. I held it in one hand and latched the leash to Tooter's harness with the other. James might not walk me to the library, but I'd follow him until we passed the library. I whispered, "Advocate for yourself."

If James was surprised to see me with my white cane, he covered it up well. I don't use it much, since I always have someone to take me wherever I want to go. But I figured I better start, especially if I was going to convince Mom and Dad I didn't need to go to a stupid special school.

The cane has a metal tip so I can feel changes in the sidewalk. James kept pace about two or three sidewalk squares ahead of me, but he didn't cross any streets until I was beside him. Not that he'd look at me or anything.

I can make out street corners and driveways, but the cane keeps me from tripping over cracks in the sidewalk or stuff people leave out, like toys or yard equipment. Our house is always super neat so that I don't trip over stuff, so it amazes me how other people don't put things away.

I kept count of how many blocks we walked (easy enough to do since Tooter stopped to pee at each intersection) and I paid attention to the curves on the path. *Tomorrow*, I thought, *I will do this myself.*

"What are you doing?" I asked James as we passed the library. He didn't pause or look up. His hands were jammed into his pockets and his hair was hanging in his face. I wondered how he could see. Maybe he needed a cane, too. Or a haircut.

"Going to the lake," he answered, annoyed.

"I know," I snapped. "But what are you doing there?"

"Don't worry about it," he sighed and raked his hands through his hair, glaring up at the sky. "I'm heading home at three o'clock. I can't stop you from following me." I almost told him I could make it fine with my cane and Tooter. But I didn't.

Inside the library, Kerica wasn't sitting in one of the hand chairs like usual. Mrs. Morris was there, though, watering the plants on the windowsill just behind the chairs. "Kerica's over by the computers," Mrs. Morris said, gesturing with her thumb toward the back of the room. I could hear the steady clicking of Kerica's fingers typing. Mrs. Morris's eyes lingered on the cane for a second.

I felt suddenly stupid holding it, like I was posing as a blind person, holding a cane and a dog's leash. I had to remind myself that I was actually blind, so it kind of made sense. Part of me wanted to fold the cane back up and shove it in my backpack, though. I let go of Tooter's leash, and he jumped up onto one of the chairs, making it after the fourth attempt. It's funny; he used to be able to make it in just one leap. Now each day it seemed to take more work to get into the same chair.

I decided to use the cane, arching it back and forth over the carpet toward the sound of the clicking. It saved my hip from banging into the edge of a bookshelf.

"Hey," Kerica said as I approached. She glanced quickly at the cane and then back to her screen.

"Hey." I pulled back the chair next to hers and sat down. "What are you doing?"

"Nothing, really." Kerica minimized the document she had been working on.

"Huh," I said. "Sounded like you were typing pretty fast for nothing."

"Oh. It's just . . ." I saw the flyer for the Sinkville Success Stories contest on the desk next to the monitor.

"Are you entering the contest?" I bounced a little in my seat. "What's your idea? Maybe we can compare notes!"

Kerica bit her lip. "Are you serious? You're really going to enter it?"

I stopped bouncing. "Yeah. Why wouldn't I?"

"Well. You just moved here and . . ."

"And what? I may have just moved here, but I can see things with a fresh perspective."

Kerica's eyes widened.

"Oh, come on!" I snapped. "It's an expression."

She sort of shrugged and turned back to the monitor. "If you want to work together, just ask."

"Huh?" She was totally losing me.

"I get that you want to enter. Everyone does," Kerica said. Her voice was suddenly the cold, crisp voice she used with Sandi. "But I'm not going to do it for you. Sandi already tried that earlier today and I told her no, too."

I folded my cane back together with quick snaps. "What are you talking about?"

"Look," Kerica turned to face me, but she didn't meet my eyes. "I've gotten burned before being partners with people on projects and doing all the work myself. I'd rather work alone."

I felt my face flame. "You don't think I can do it alone?"

"I think you're going to need a lot of help. And I'm not . . . I don't—"

"I get it," I snapped. "You work alone. Guess what? Me, too."

Kerica stared at me. "You're seriously going to try to do this on your own? You don't even know the town. You just moved here! All you know about Sinkville is your home and the library. That can't be a success story."

It was on the tip of my tongue to say that I also had been to the Williams Diner. "Why are you being such a jerk?" I said instead.

"Why won't you admit that you're totally going to need me to do all of the work for you?" Kerica's voice lowered into a hiss. "My mom already lectured me about it the whole drive here. First, I have to be nice to Sandi even though she's never nice to anyone, just because she's one of Mom's students. Now, I've got to help you with this project, just because you're . . ."

"I'm what?" Now my voice was just as cold as Kerica's.

She sighed and rolled her eyes. "Because you're blind and sad."

I whipped my folded cane into a straight line with way more force than necessary and slammed my sunhat back on my head. "I never asked you to do anything for me. And just for the record, I wouldn't want to work with you on the project. You're too bossy and too much of a snob!"

Mrs. Morris stepped toward me as I rushed from the children's section, dragging Tooter by his leash. Tooter's back legs went limp so I scooped him up under my arm and kept walking.

Mrs. Morris had a bunch of books in her hand and a kid trailing her. He was asking for everything on local history and successful businesses. Another essay writer. But Mrs. Morris wasn't listening to the kid. "Kerica?" I heard her half-question, half-yell.

I paused by Mrs. Dexter at the front desk. Trying not to breathe in her perfume of rotting lavender, I asked how to get to the lake. Still talking like I was deaf instead of blind—extra loud and slowly—she gave me directions.

"Wait! Shouldn't I tell your dog?" she called as I stormed out of the library.

Maybe Part One of Sinkville Success Stories would be on the shores of the lake. Or at least maybe I'd find out what James had been up to lately.

"Hey!" a shaky voice called just as I got my cell phone out to call James. I was so startled, I dropped the phone. Using the cane, I found it without having to go on my hands and knees. I bent, picked it up, and turned toward the voice. I squinted through my darkened lenses.

Luckily, it wasn't too bright today, but I guess I was more nervous than I thought about venturing out solo because everything was pretty scattered. I had followed Mrs. Dexter's directions to take the sidewalk from the library, to cross the street, and to turn onto a dirt pathway cutting though a wooded area to the lake. I saw the bluish-gray water stretched out to my left and breathed in the algae and fishy smell. The lake was a lot bigger than I had thought it would be.

I couldn't see the shore well. I could go down to the shoreline and maybe have a better chance of finding James. (Think how impressed he'd be that I got here alone!) But I'd also have a much better chance of getting hopelessly lost if I went off the path. The cane would keep me from tripping. But would it keep me from totally losing any sense of direction? Not so much. So I was about to do the unforgivable—call James (think about how annoyed he'd be that he had to rescue me!)—when I heard the voice.

"James?" I called back, even though the shaky voice didn't sound anything like my brother's.

"Nah," the voice, closer now, replied. Then I saw a man curled around a wooden cane like a comma, taking small, tired steps in my direction. A couple strides and he was beside me. Just like I had thought, it was the old whittler man from the Williams Diner.

"Well, now," he said, leaning heavily on his cane. "It's my gnome girl."

"Hi!" I said, feeling my face split into a grin. I pulled the gnome out of my pocket and showed it to him. "This *is* lucky!"

The lake wasn't supposed to be there.

Mr. Hamlin, the old whittler, told me so in a voice softer than the water that lapped against my feet. We sat on a dock that stretched out over the lake, Tooter curled against me snoring. Mr. Hamlin sat in a folding chair with peeling plastic weaving. A small blade in his right hand ate at a lump of wood cupped in his left. The curling strips that fell around him reminded me of getting my hair cut.

Mr. Hamlin said the lake used to be farmland. "If you were to walk over that way," he said, not looking up from the wood but throwing out his curled hand toward the left, "you'd see what looks like a road going straight into the water. That's my old driveway."

M. H. Bartel Paper Company apparently needed a body of water to draw from during operations. They purchased about a half-dozen farms, the Hamlin property included. All in all, the lake totaled a couple hundred acres. "Town needed jobs," Mr. Hamlin said. "I had just gotten the farm from my papa. That Bartel money was more than I'd make in a decade of farming. Didn't think too much 'bout it. Signed the paper."

He sighed, flipping the wood around in his hand. I noticed he barely looked at his whittling. The wood was mostly covered in his hand. The knife just seemed to see on its own where it should dodge, where it should gauge. Mr. Hamlin shifted in his creaking chair. A bird called out over the water, and I pictured it swooping in and catching fish.

"Are there fish in there? If the lake is fake, I mean?" The water stretched so wide and long I couldn't see the other shore. I could hear a motorboat in the distance. It seemed crazy to think this water hadn't always been here, that water this deep and wide could've been put here by people.

"Oh, yeah," Mr. Hamlin half-laughed. "They added fish same way they added water. By the truck-full. Toads, frogs, birds, all of 'em came along soon after."

Mr. Hamlin said that when the lake was being filled, he already was a dad. He had held his wiggly baby in his arms, standing far back along the future shoreline as the trucks pulled in. They lined up around the land, the farmhouse still standing in the middle, where his grandfather had built it. One by one, each trucker pulled out a hose and sprayed fresh water onto the land. The water churned and spread, going from a puddle around the house until it lapped at the sides. Soon, the water seemed to suck down the farmhouse, gnawing up, up, up around its wooden sides. For a long time, only the peaked roof could be seen. By then, Mr. Hamlin said, he didn't realize he was crying until his tears splashed against the baby's sleeping head.

"I thought I had to have forgotten somethin' in the house. I almost yelled at them to stop, to let me go back in, even though I knew I couldn't." Mr. Hamlin's voice stayed steady and soft, like this was a bedtime story he had read aloud so many times he couldn't be bothered making the various character voices anymore. I squeezed my eyes shut to picture it. "I knew better. We had combed through the house. Everything of value was packed up, waiting to be unpacked once our new house was built. Our new lakeshore house," Mr. Hamlin chuckled.

That's when he remembered, he said. The wall outside his old bedroom—where the nursery had been just a few days earlier. That's where he had scrawled MIKE HAMLIN WAS HERE when he was seven. The knife had slipped and ended up stabbing his palm. "Still have the scar," he said, holding up his hand. I pretended to see it.

He remembered, too, the spot on the edge of the brick hearth. That's where he stepped every morning on the way to the kitchen. No real reason for stepping there. It just felt right when he did, not right when he didn't.

The little herb garden on the patch of land just by the back door—that's the only spot where he could still picture his mom, who had died when he was eleven. In his mind, she was moving among the raised bed with a small pair of scissors, humming while she thought of making her famous carrot and thyme soup.

He had wished he had taken the kitchen sink. It's where his baby, the one he held in his arms as the water rose, had gotten his first bath. It's where he had his first bath, too.

"All gone," Mr. Hamlin said. "All at the bottom of this lake like a sunken treasure."

This time, I was surprised to find myself crying. I scooted over and put my hand on Mr. Hamlin's shoulder.

"Ah, stop blubbering," he chuckled. "I got me a job at the Mill. Let the other twenty acres go farrow and became a paper man. That and this lake let me send that baby o'mine to college. Can you imagine it? That land never grew anything more than farmers. Never college kids. Never lawyers. Now my son helps people, defends them in court, makes sure there's justice served. Wouldn't have happened without this here lake."

Mr. Hamlin looked up over the water. A small smile spread across his wrinkled tan cheeks. "My grandbaby, only fifteen but gonna graduate this year. College is next. Wants to own a farm, but one for horses and free-range chickens and pigs. Her daddy? He doesn't want to hear it. He plans to sell the leftover land and settle me in a home."

"A home? Don't you have a home already?" I asked.

He smiled. "He means an old folks' home, where I'll get wheeled around, sponge bathed on Tuesdays, and have creamed carrots shoveled down my throat at every meal. No more whittling, no more young girls popping in out of the woods, no more nothing."

"That sounds terrible!"

"I'm not doing it, don't worry. He gets grouchier about it every year. Talks about how I fell on my hip last summer and no one knew I couldn't get up for a day. He brings up my asthma, too." Mr. Hamlin blew on the chunk of wood in his hand and chuckled.

I chewed my lip. "Maybe you could have someone check in on you?"

"My grandbaby, she checks in now and again. But her daddy and I don't always see things eye to eye."

"I'll check on you," I promised.

Mr. Hamlin laughed. "Gnome Girl, you remind me of Sarah, my grandbaby. Funny, isn't it? She just wants to farm. All those brains. All those opportunities. And she just wants to have the rest of the old Hamlin land and work it again. Things go round, you know?"

He opened his palm to show me that lump of wood. Only now it was a top.

"Mr. Hamlin?" I asked as the laps of water ticked out a few minutes of silence. I pulled out an old reporter's notebook of Mom's—one that I found in the still-unpacked boxes outside her bedroom door—and a pencil from my backpack and flipped it to a blank page. "Can I write down your story?"

Mr. Hamlin chuckled. "You entering that contest, Gnome Girl?"

I nodded, my pencil already scribbling things about the lake and Mr. Hamlin's house.

"Don't know how my flooded house was a success, but you go ahead."

Chapter Six

For a long time, I sat by Mr. Hamlin's feet and played with the wooden top on the dock. My mind spun along with the toy, trying to make sense of the sacrifice Mr. Hamlin had made by giving up his farm. I thought about how he didn't realize how hard it would be to let go until it sank away. For some reason, it made me think of Mom.

Since Mom was a travel writer, I bet she could create a Sinkville contest entry in minutes, scouting out stories and pulling them together. Heck, she could probably do it with her eyes shut. (That idea sort of made me laugh out loud, making Mr. Hamlin shift in his creaky chair.) I should be working on the essay with her—after all, I had an expert right in my own house—instead of wandering around with a cane, leading a fat farting dog and talking to an old man with fake teeth.

The top whirled again. Was Mom really that same fearless reporter she once had been? She had traveled all over the world and it was no big deal. So moving to

South Carolina shouldn't have been, either, only it was. Going to the library made her exhausted. She hadn't left her bedroom since. Why couldn't she be strong for me? Why couldn't she stop being so depressed?

"Mind goin' over to the woods there about and g'ttin' me another block of wood to work on?" Mr. Hamlin asked, scattering my thoughts.

He told me he wanted something interesting and small. He said I'd find something near the shore, where wood was softened by the water. "I'm not lookin' to make anything special. Just want to keep my hands busy a while," he said.

My cane tapped the debris along the water's edge. I ignored the higher pitched taps of rocks. When I heard the quieter thud of the cane hitting wood, I bent down. A large pine branch had broken into pieces. I combed through the pieces on my hands and knees, piling a few beside me. Tooter, his leash dragging behind him, sniffed at the wood.

"Don't you pee on these," I warned him. I wasn't sure exactly what Mr. Hamlin wanted, but they looked like they might be good for whittling.

I folded up the bottom of my shirt to cradle the wood and held it in place with my left arm. I held the cane in my right hand and zeroed in on Mr. Hamlin, who hadn't stopped whistling since I stepped off the dock.

I had just stepped up onto the trail when Tooter growled softly toward the woods. Suddenly the branches in front of me split and out thrashed my brother. "James!" I squealed.

"Alice?" He sounded shocked. His arm shot out to the side, the way Dad's does when he brakes suddenly while driving. A girl pushed his arm aside and stepped forward. As she got closer, I saw it was Mr. Hamlin's granddaughter.

"Hey!" she said. Now that she was closer, I could see she was holding a huge frog. "I know you. You're the Williams Diner girl."

"No, *you're* the Williams Diner girl." I smiled.

"You know her?" James asked, turning his head from the girl to me and back.

"I'm Alice," I said. I put my hand out to shake. The girl shifted the frog to the other hand and shook my hand. Hers was cold and dirty.

"I'm Sarah," she said. She didn't even glance at my cane. I liked that about her.

I wasn't sure, though, that I liked the look James gave her . . . or me.

"What are you doing here?" James asked.

I shrugged. "I got sick of the library so I decided to check out the lake."

"Who's with you?" James rushed forward, pushing back my sunhat and looking at my face. Then he ran his

83

hand down my arms, pressing the white skin to make sure it wasn't burned. It's what Mom did whenever she worried I had gotten too much sun. Sunburns are a little tricky with me. Sometimes I don't look red but my arms break out in hives later, like I'm allergic to the sun. But I had been sitting in Mr. Hamlin's shade, so I wasn't burned at all.

"I'm fine, James." I pulled my arm back. "Got to get this wood back to Mr. Hamlin."

I turned and walked toward the dock, fighting the urge to jump in the air a little.

Turns out, James spent less time at the lake than he did following Sarah around, at least according to Mr. Hamlin. Sarah had a thing for animals. Mr. Hamlin said she spent most of the summer going around catching frogs and watching birds. That is, when she wasn't volunteering at Sinkville Animal Care, the local veterinary and animal rescue. His voice was different when he talked about Sarah. It reminded me of when I overheard Dad talking to other grown-ups about James scoring at basketball games.

We were now all sitting in rockers on Mr. Hamlin's front porch. Once the sun was in the middle of the sky, it got too hot and too bright for the dock, so we had packed up and moved. Tooter lay beside me, staring suspiciously at the rocking chair and bristling a little every time it went back and then forward again.

After the lake swallowed Mr. Hamlin's family farmhouse, he told me he had built a white bungalow with a wraparound porch. He rocked and carved on that porch, the chunks of wood I had gathered piled atop the pieces he already had stacked within hand's reach by his chair. My rocking chair creaked three or four times for every steady groan emitting from his.

"What do you mean 'he has it bad'?"

"Well, look at him." Then Mr. Hamlin, without missing a beat, launched into describing how James was following at Sarah's heels as she walked the borders of what was left of Hamlin's farmland. "She's looking at the land like its blooming. He's looking at her the same way."

I closed my eyes, imagining it. I felt myself smile. "What does it look like? The land when it's a working farm?"

"Huh," the old man said. "Working is the right word for it. That's all I ever saw when it was mine. Nothing but weeds that needed pulling. Plots that needed plowing. Crops that needed harvesting. Nothing but work, work, work." *Creak, creak, creak* from his chair. "But my papa? He saw nothing but possibilities, a circle of growth. He would stand on the porch and look over the growth like, well, like your brother is looking at my grandbaby."

"He's got it bad," I echoed.

"Sure do."

Much later, as the late afternoon sun stood just above the treetops surrounding the lake, James and I made our way home.

"What are you smiling about?" James smirked. I hadn't even realized I was smiling until he said that. But once he did, I found I couldn't stop. Finally I figured out what was making me so happy and it wasn't just meeting Mr. Hamlin again.

"You found something you like about Sinkville," I sing-songed. "Or at least some*one* you like. Ooo-la-la!"

"Shut up." James's cheeks flushed.

"It's okay. You can like it here. I won't tell."

"Shut up," James said again. His lips twitched like he was trying not to smile.

But with each step that took us closer to our Sinkville home, James's face shuttered. Gone was the open face, soft eyes, and twitching lips of a boy maybe in love, and it was replaced with the slouching stance and bitter glares of my brother. As we reached the front door, his arm shot out, gripping me by the elbow. "Don't tell Mom," he said, his voice urgent.

"Tell her what?"

"About . . . you know." His eyes darted so fast across my face that I would've sworn he was the one with nystagmus.

"Sarah?" I smiled at him. "I don't think Mom would make fun of you. She'd be glad to know you're happy. Ouch!"

James's grip suddenly tightened. "No!" he said, but then he lowered his hand.

"James? James. Mom *wants* us to be happy. She told me."

He shoved his hands through his hair, gripping the ends and shaking his head. "You don't get it."

"No," I answered to his back as he shoved by me into the house. "I guess I don't."

Chapter Seven

*M*om *once told* me that one of her travel assignments was to get "an insider's guide" to boutique shopping in Paris. Mom knew she could go into any one of the shops lining the Champs-Élysées, tell the owner that she was a journalist, and soon be pampered like a queen. But she wanted to hold true to the insider's aspect, to find out where a rich local woman would go and how she would be treated. So Mom sipped a fancy coffee at an outdoor bistro overlooking the paved footpath as wide as a road. She waited for the perfect example of a posh Parisian to pass by. She didn't have to wait long.

Passing by on six-inch stilettos was a tall, thin woman. Her hair fell in perfect glossy waves down the middle of her back. She carried a purse slung over her shoulder that cost more than Mom's transcontinental flight tickets. A small bag with tissue paper and the Cartier label swung from her manicured hand.

Mom trailed several feet behind the woman, making note of the stores she entered and those she skipped. When the woman turned off the main footpath, Mom quickened her step. A few moments later the woman emerged from an amazing perfumery. Mom jotted down the address, eager to check it out but not willing to lose her "insider."

A few blocks and several boutiques later, Mom panicked. While she was scribbling notes about the last shop in her notebook, the woman disappeared! Mom turned in a slow circle, looking for the posh Parisian. Suddenly she heard a crass, "Hey! Hey, you!" in an angry Southern drawl.

Mom turned toward the yell and was face-to-face with the posh Parisian once more. "All of Paris," (she pronounced it *Pear-eee*), "and you gotta follow me? You got a problem with 'Mericans?"

Soon Mom realized she had been following a stay-at-home mom from Georgia checking out the famous shopping boulevard for the first time. Even more ironic, the woman thought *Mom* was a Parisian.

"So much for an insider's guide," Mom had said at the end of her story.

For some reason, I recalled this whenever I tucked my Sinkville Success Stories notebook in my back pocket. Probably most kids' contest essays would be on the paper mill or the town leaders. But maybe Sinkville's best success stories weren't so obvious.

One morning, James headed toward the lake and I inched toward the library doors with feet that felt weighted down like Mr. Hamlin's drowned house. And not just because Tooter kept stopping to pee on each and every crack in the sidewalk. I swear, he peed more every day. The sun beat down on my sunhat and I felt my forehead bead with sweat. But I'd take two steps toward the library, then turn and take one step back toward the lake, even though my mind echoed with James's hissed warning that I needed to give him "some freaking space." I guess I'd been spending a lot of time at the lake with Mr. Hamlin. I now had a gnome, a top, a rocking chair, and a boat sitting on top of my dresser. James seemed to think I was just spying on him and Sarah, though.

That was completely unfair. First of all, the obvious. Blind people aren't known for their spy skills. Secondly, I *liked* that James was spending time with Sarah. The more time he spent with her, the less he concentrated on showing Dad that Sinkville stunk.

Sure, he was a complete jerk about pointing out the sunburn I had gotten yesterday. Mr. Hamlin was so into whittling that little boat—and doing such an awesome job of describing the real one in the distance he was using as inspiration—that I sort of ignored the fact that my skin was feeling a little bubbly. By the time we moved to the porch an hour later, my arms were pinker than Tooter's tongue and just as bumpy. I had teeny tiny blisters all over. No big deal, really. But James must've pointed them out a half-dozen times at dinner.

"Did you know skin cancer is the fastest growing cancer among young people?" he had said, like he was talking about baseball scores. "So many people around here look like their skin is made of leather. And you know sun damage can never be reversed."

His attempt failed, though. Dad didn't jump up and start packing boxes. Mom didn't cry for Seattle. In fact, she and Dad had a hushed conversation about a doctor's appointment and an increase in medication. I thought at first they meant for me, but I soon figured out that Mom was talking about herself. It seemed to make both of them smile a little.

That night, Mom smeared my arms with aloe vera and made me promise to stay out of the sun the next day. "And wear your long-sleeve cotton dress," she said.

I crinkled my nose and was about to say, "No way," but then I had a better idea. "Okay. And you be sure to read the newspaper in the morning."

She tilted her head at me, confused. But I had a plan of my own. I'd been getting up super early every morning and using my magnifier to read the part of the newspaper that had job postings. I started with just putting that section in front, but I had moved on to circling the listings that I thought she'd be great at doing, like dog grooming, delivering newspapers, and truck driving. There were even a few ads for freelance writing. I remembered what Dad had said about how going back to work stopped her depression when James was a baby and about how having a cause halted it when I was born. Maybe this would help now.

Before James and I left that morning, I circled six jobs.

"Good-bye," James said with a little too much force on the "bye" part when I didn't move quickly toward the library doors.

I knew he'd be furious if I went to the lake. Even worse, I knew Mr. Hamlin would be disappointed to see me. Not because he didn't like me. I knew that he did. But he wanted me to patch things up with Kerica.

Mr. Hamlin listened to all my stories just like I listened to his, only lately his stories were all about times he avoided stuff and it knocked him "up the rear and back again." Then he'd stop rocking in his chair, narrow his eyes at me, and ask about Kerica. I had told all about the fall-out with Eliza, and maybe he thought I should have at least one friend my age.

And maybe I had been avoiding Kerica. So what? She had been such a jerk to me. I turned back toward the lake. But then again, she had been my only friend for weeks. I shouldn't just give up on her. I took a few more steps toward the library.

I was almost to the doors when two things happened at once: Tooter let out a scary long, low growl and someone called out, "Are you lost?" over the hedge. Like a groundhog popping out of a hole in the ground, Sandi's head suddenly appeared.

"Ah, hi, Sandi," I said. "No, I'm just letting Tooter go potty before we go inside."

"Huh," Sandi replied. "Looked to me like you were trying to decide whether to go inside." I stepped closer to the hedge and saw that she had a blanket stretched out on the grass on the other side. A pile of books lay beside her, but none were open. Sandi lay back on the blanket, pulling up her shorts so they were more like bikini bottoms. She adjusted her tank top straps. Something about the way she wiggled her legs made me think of bacon browning in a pan.

"You know suntanning is really bad for you, right?"

"Being whiter than paper is bad for you, too. At least, it is socially," she said back.

I sucked in my breath, too shocked to reply.

"I wouldn't blame you, you know," she said, "about not wanting to go inside. Kerica is being even more of a jerk than usual." Sandi rose up on one elbow and lowered her oversized sunglasses so she could peek at me over the top. "Do you know she actually told me to shut up today? Seriously. All I did was ask her to type up some notes for me. I mean, she clearly has no social plans. She has the time."

What a jerk! I thought, and mentally fist bumped Kerica for saying no to Sandi. But really I just pulled Tooter's leash back. His fur bristled and he growled at Sandi again. "Notes about the Sinkville Success Stories contest?" I managed to squeak out.

"Yeah," said Sandi. A cloud of coconut tanning oil slapped me in the face when she readjusted herself on the blanket. "My mom has made contact with the mayor, the state representative, and the senator that represents our area. We're trying to reach the governor, too. And Mom has important contacts with the Bartel family. I'm going to showcase how the Mill has 'churned out' success for fifty years. Get it? Churned! It's totally going to blow away all the other stupid essays, like Brian Thomas's profile on M. H. Bartel. How original. So, um, what's your angle?" she asked as she dropped her sunglasses down her nose and peered over them at me.

"I'm sort of going a different route. Talking to more residents, I guess." Suddenly I saw how stupid my idea was. Of course, Sinkville's success was the Mill, not someone who saw his house drown. Here I was interviewing a whittler while she was talking to senators. Lame.

"Hmm," Sandi said, like she could read my thoughts. "Well, don't go asking Kerica for help typing. I doubt Kerica would help you even if you played the blind card."

Blind card? My mind snagged on the words but Sandi kept right on blabbing. "I guess I can't expect more than that. She's always had a problem with me. Jealousy." Sandi flopped onto her side on the blanket.

"I don't think that's it," I blurted without thinking.

Sandi didn't seem to take offense, though.

"Of course that's it," she said. "She's been bitter and mean ever since last year. To think, we were even partners in science class."

Something about this tickled my mind. When Kerica had freaked out about the Sinkville Success Stories project, she had said something about partner work not being good for her.

"Did you work on some project together?" I swear, I had been struck with a sudden case of diarrhea of the mouth. There's no other explanation for continuing this conversation with Sandi.

Sandi repositioned her sunglasses and directed her face toward the sun. "Did she tell you about that? I'm not surprised." Sandi sighed. "It was just a simple science project. Could be on anything. The big brains in there decided it should be about DNA extraction. For reals! For a fifth-grade science project! And then Kerica totally lost it because our styles are different." Sandi flipped over to her back. "I'm more of a wing-it type of personality. And I have a *life*. So I didn't 'pull my weight.' Whatever. We didn't *fail*."

"But you didn't get a good grade?" Again. Mouth diarrhea.

"It wasn't a true *partnership* according to the teacher. It was too one-sided."

I had a good guess which side did all of the work.

"We got a C. So what? C's are passing." Sandi flicked a fly away. "But Kerica freaked out. Tried to blame *me* for compromising her scholarship. Said if she had to go back to public school in Columbia, it'd be completely my fault. But, really, it's like the teacher said. She should've been more of a leader."

I felt my forehead crinkle as I worked through what Sandi was telling me. "Wait a sec—what scholarship?"

"Kerica only goes to school here because her mom tutors M. H. Bartel students. And, yeah, because of her stellar GPA."

"M. H. Bartel? The paper mill?"

"No, silly," Sandi giggled. "The school. M. H. Bartel School for Girls."

"But I thought the school was called Sinkville Public?"

"Yes, the public school is *Sinkville Public*," Sandi answered like Mrs. Dexter, slowly as if I might not understand her words. "But M. H. Bartel is a private school."

"So, I wouldn't be in the same school as you and Kerica even if I did go to the public school?" Tooter pulled on his leash, sniffling around for a spot to do his business. I dropped it, figuring he wouldn't go far.

Sandi giggled again. "No. Kerica doesn't even live in Sinkville, first of all. Secondly, M. H. Bartel is very exclusive. They won't let just anyone in. My mom is an alumna. She says M. H. Bartel is world renowned. She'd know. In fact, maybe I'll get her to score an interview with the director for the con—"

"Oh no!" I yelled, pushing through the hedge and cutting off Sandi's sentence. "Stop, Tooter! Stop! Do not pee on Sandi's—!"

"Oh my God!" Sandi screamed as a stream of Tooter pee hit her leg. She shoved him away, but the dumb dog just stood there, kicking grass on an already outraged Sandi.

Tooter actually scraped Sandi's shin when he put his foot down. Sandi held her leg and howled, but I doubted it hurt that much. I snagged up his leash and tried to choke out an apology, but Tooter just pranced in the direction of the library. He looked back over his shoulder slowly, not at all bothered by Sandi's screams, waiting for me to catch up.

"See you later, Sandi," I said, matching Tooter's casual stance.

I held it together until the glass doors closed behind me. "Ha!" I screeched as Tooter twirled in circles in front of me. "You wicked, wicked fur ball of awesomesauce!"

Tooter rolled onto his back, his tongue flapping out to the side, so, of course, I sunk down to my knees to rub his belly. "You little genius!"

"That is the most unusual service animal," Mrs. Dexter called from behind her cloud of lavender-mill scent.

Ignoring her, I said to Tooter, "Okay, lead the way to Kerica."

He dutifully hopped up, scooted his butt across the floor a few inches, and pranced toward the children's section.

"Most unusual," I heard Mrs. Dexter murmur.

Kerica sat in front of the computer again, but her fingers weren't flying across the keys. They lay in her lap while she stared toward the hand chairs. I had dropped the leash as soon as I had seen her, and Tooter scrambled toward Kerica. She squealed a little when Tooter leaped up onto her lap and licked at her chin. "Tooter! What are you doing here?"

I smiled, thinking of the contrast between Tooter's reception for Sandi and this one for Kerica. "He's with me," I said and pulled out the chair next to Kerica's.

She flashed me a quick smile. "I'm glad you're here," she said, burying her face a little in Tooter's side. "I wanted to tell you . . . the way I acted . . ."

Sorry didn't seem to be something Kerica was used to saying, seeing as she had trouble getting out the words. "It's okay," I said. "I think it was probably a misunderstanding. I ran into Sandi outside . . ."

Then I told Kerica about what Sandi had said about the school project gone bad. "Sounds like you ended up having to do all the work. I'd be skittish about starting another group project after that, too," I said.

"Thanks," Kerica said, "but I shouldn't have said all that stuff. And if you want—"

I interrupted. "I don't want to work together. I mean, no offense or anything. I just really want to do it by myself. I already have a couple ideas."

"It turns out that I can't enter. You have to live in Sinkville, and I live in Columbia." Kerica's fingers twisted in Tooter's fur. I swear, the mixed-up dog started to purr. "I'm not eligible."

"I'm sorry. I bet that's hard, spending all your time here and living somewhere else. Have you thought about moving?"

Kerica shook her head. "My grandma lives with us and she has all these friends in the city. She doesn't like the idea of small towns like this. Thinks they're filled with mean, close-minded people. She goes to the community center almost every day. Mom said it'd break Grandma's heart to move. Plus it costs a lot more for an apartment here than there. Librarians don't make a lot of money, you know."

"Oh," I said.

Her fingers kept twisting Tooter's fur. "It's tough. I mean, half my life is there in Columbia. Half here in this stupid library or, during the school year, Bartel School for Girls. But I'm never really at home anywhere." Tooter stood on Kerica's lap and twirled around once, probably to dislodge her fingers from pulling on his fur.

"What do you mean?" I asked.

Kerica clenched her teeth and flexed her fingers. She reminded me, for some reason, of James. It looked like it actually hurt to open up a little. But I bet it hurt more to keep it all inside. I scooted my chair a little closer to her. "At home, I don't fit in because I don't go to that school. Here I don't fit in because it's not my home."

"I felt like that when we moved here. My whole life was back in Seattle but I was here. I really wanted to move back."

"Wanted to?" Kerica asked. "So you don't anymore?"

I shrugged. "Well, I got into a big fight with my best friend there, Eliza. She's sort of moved on, I guess. Made a bunch of new friends."

Kerica nodded.

"But I made a new best friend, too." I elbowed Kerica.

Her smile was slow, like it took a long time for my words to reach her ears. "I'm your best friend?"

I nodded.

"I don't think I've had a best friend before," she whispered.

"Well, you do now."

"Even though I said those stupid, mean things to you?"

"Yeah," I said. "Friends can get mad at each other and still make up." I took a deep breath. Maybe it wasn't so easy for me to say how I feel, either. "I know what it's like to feel different. But you're not alone. Okay? Want to do something different today?" I said to change the subject. "I got my allowance yesterday. We could go do anything!"

"I don't know," Kerica murmured. "I just started this book . . ."

"And let me guess, you've only read three so far this month?"

Kerica grinned. "Six."

"Gah!" I said. "Let's get out of here before you read the dictionaries! Are we close to that milkshake place?"

"The Williams Diner?" Kerica asked. "It's only about four or five blocks from here."

I nodded. "I'll tell you about the shower Sandi got this morning while we walk."

Chapter Eight

Kerica couldn't stop laughing. She bent over and held her stomach, bellowing laughs like a dying donkey. "You have no idea how much I would've loved to have seen Tooter pee on her! Do you think he'd do it again? Like maybe it could be his trick. Someone makes you mad and Super Tooter to the rescue!"

I laughed and rubbed Tooter's head. "I kind of feel bad about it. He sort of scratched her leg with his nails."

I looked for a place to tie Tooter's leash outside the diner, but Kerica grabbed the leash from me. "I'm buying this guy a hamburger."

"Hang on!" I called to her as she and Tooter walked in. "I don't think dogs can go in there!"

This time I was ready for Grandma's voice to come out of Gretel's mouth. But it made my knees wobbly. "Hey there, sweetheart," she said. One of her electric blue fingernails pointed to an empty booth. "We'll make an exception for the pup this one time, since the lunch crowd's gone for the day. You ladies here for a treat?"

"Kerica and I'd like some milkshakes."

"Be careful," Gretel chuckled. "Milkshake addiction might run in your blood."

"I'll take my chances," I said. I asked her to whip up whatever she had made for Dad that morning.

"Which time? His first order was a kale and berry smoothie. An hour later, he came back for a peanut butter shake."

"Peanut butter!" I said.

Kerica ordered a strawberry shake with a plain hamburger on the side for Tooter.

As Gretel turned to walk away, I asked, "Any chance you can add a little coconut and maybe some jelly to mine?"

Gretel grinned. "That's a combo I haven't had before. Going to make one for myself, too." The back of the menu had the Williams Diner history printed on it. Kerica read it out loud while I took notes in my reporter's notebook.

When Gretel brought out our shakes a few minutes later, I saw she really had made one for herself, too. Gretel wiped her painted-pink lips with a napkin. "Golly, girl," she said as she handed me my shake. "That's delicious! Never would've thought to add coconut."

"My mom used to make PB&J with coconut sandwiches," I said around a gulp of creamy goodness.

"Well, your mom's creation just got added to our menu." She handed Kerica her shake and said, "Reading up on our history?"

Kerica slurped her milkshake, licked her lips, and nodded. "Yeah, I'm up to the nineteen sixties."

"What's with the notebook?" asked Gretel while I finished scribbling some notes.

"She's entering the Sinkville Success Stories contest," Kerica answered for me since my mouth was full of milkshake.

"This diner? A success story?" Gretel made a humpfing sound.

"No, really," I said as soon as I could swallow without getting brain freeze. "This is good information!"

"How 'bout you, sweetie?" Gretel asked Kerica. "You putting this dinky diner in your essay?"

This time, I answered for Kerica. "She can't enter. It's only for Sinkville residents."

"I didn't realize," Gretel said. "Sorry, Kerica."

Kerica shrugged. "It's no big deal." She picked up an extra pencil I had left on the table and doodled on the paper placemat.

Gretel scanned the restaurant and tilted her head toward the counter. A person was talking loudly into a cell phone. Once I heard the booming voice—"That's right! The smell of success!"—I figured out who it was: Mayor Hank.

"Harold over there is the one to ask for Sinkville's real history from the sixties on," Gretel said as she sank into the booth beside me. "Might give you some insight into this contest, too. You ladies know all about the civil rights movement here in Sinkville, I'm sure."

Kerica nodded, but I shook my head. "I'm from Seattle," I reminded them.

They rolled their eyes at me in unison and I had to laugh. Gretel said, "In the early sixties, life was a lot different here in the South. Some places—railroad stations, doctors' waiting rooms, lunch counters in the city—they didn't serve anyone who was black."

"Or they made us sit in a different room, come in through a different entrance, even drink from a different water fountain." Kerica didn't look up from her sketch while she talked. I leaned closer to see what she was drawing, but it just looked like blurs to me. "Grandma talks about it a lot."

Gretel nodded. "It was a dark, cruel time. The sad thing is, I wasn't even aware of it. It wasn't until the civil rights movement—when people, mostly young people, protested the laws—that I even began to give it some thought."

Kerica's face was screwed up like she was fighting to keep something inside.

"It's okay, honey, you go ahead and say what you need to say," Gretel said softly.

"My grandma never stops thinking about it. Mom keeps telling her things are different now but she won't move from our neighborhood. She never stopped thinking about it."

Gretel reached toward Kerica, putting her wrinkled hand over Kerica's smooth one. Kerica kept sketching with her right hand. "I'm sorry about that, kiddo. I really am."

Tooter whimpered and licked at their joined hands.

"Williams Diner didn't make African Americans sit somewhere else, did they?" I asked.

"No," Gretel shook her head. "Daddy never would've done that. But the thing is, even though we didn't have a law about it, or one of those awful 'Whites Only' signs in the front window, there were so many unwritten laws. Customs that people followed even if they weren't enforced."

"Like black people only shopping on Saturdays," Kerica said. "Grandma still only shops on Saturdays."

Gretel nodded. "And that if a white person owned a diner, black people would go to a different one. So even though Dad would've whipped up a milkshake for anyone who came in our doors, no one of color would. Until Harold changed things."

Gretel took another drink of her milkshake. "See that man over there?" Even though I couldn't make out

Mayor Hank from where I sat, with my eyes closed I could paint a picture of him. I saw his belly pushing at the buttons of his striped shirt. His hands full of flyers for the Sinkville Success Stories contest. His cheeks red and eyes scanning. "Now take away fifty years and just as many pounds. Maybe a few more."

Suddenly I saw a young man, shirt sleeves pulled up to show muscled arms. I saw eyes bright and chin set. "He was handsome," I murmured.

"That he was," Gretel said. I peeked and saw that her eyes were closed, too.

In a soft voice, she continued: "In nineteen sixty-four, the Civil Rights Act passed. Harold there was a teenage busboy working for my dad. For months he had been talking about the movement, about department stores closing rather than serving black men and women at the lunch counter. He wanted to join the sit-ins and protests, but his mama wouldn't let him. Said he was too young. But Harold supported the movement in ways that didn't put him in danger. Even took on the role as manager, setting up meetings in safe places."

"A lot of people got hurt during that time," Kerica piped in. "That's why my grandma's still scared. People were beat by police officers, had rocks thrown at them. Some were arrested for no reason."

"In other parts of the South, it was even worse," Gretel said. "Some people died. But Harold had to do something. That's just the way he is. When he sees a way to make our town better, he has to do it. But I thought for sure he'd give my dad a heart attack with what he did!"

"What did he do?" Kerica and I asked together.

Gretel grinned. "He went to that big window at the front of the store." Gretel thumbed behind her. The window was huge, covering most of one wall of the restaurant. "He painted on it the most enormous set of hands you've ever seen. One white hand, one black hand, shaking. Under it, he wrote in huge letters, EVERYONE WELCOME AT WILLIAMS."

I felt my forehead wrinkle. "Why would your dad be mad about that? Didn't he support the movement?"

Gretel laughed, her cheeks turning rosy. "He was in favor of equal rights, for sure. But he also was in favor of someone having a smidge of artistic talent before painting his storefront windows!"

Her laughter wheezed between her words. "You should've seen those sad-looking claws Harold painted. Picture this: his first try looked more like baby paws clutching at each other. Then he reworked it, painting right over the first attempt. This time, it looked more like we were welcoming visiting aliens. The fingers

111

alone where three times the size of the arms! He tried again—and soon the entire window was covered with a pair of gigantic, and I mean *gigantic*, drippy monster claws grasping at each other." Both Kerica and I joined in Gretel's hiccuping laughs. "That man, I've seen him convince a toddler to eat a plate of brussels sprouts. But he can't paint a smiley face—let alone a handshake— worth a darn!"

Gretel wiped tears off her cheeks with a napkin. "Dad was a good man. He poured his life into this diner, making sure it supported Mama and me. But he was a slow man. Took him months to ponder menu changes." Slowly, Gretel shifted her head to look over at Mayor Hank. She tilted her head to where he sat. "Harold, he's always been a bolt of lightning. Can you imagine how Dad felt when he saw the entire front of his store painted like that?"

"Did your dad fire him?" Kerica asked, concern in her voice.

Gretel smiled. "Like I said, most times Dad was slow to move. But even he couldn't resist Harold. The world was a'changin', and Harold was one of its champions."

Gretel told us that by the end of that day, the three of them had managed to scrub the window clean. Then Gretel and her dad painted the window themselves, with Harold handling the sales inside. "Once the window was painted, Dad, Harold, and me, we just stood back and admired it. Dad went inside and grabbed his camera." She flipped the menu over to the timeline again.

I got out my magnifier from my pocket and looked at the black and white picture. Sure enough, it showed a beautiful painting of two hands shaking, welcoming everyone to the diner. A pretty girl held a paintbrush in front of it, a small smile on her face. Next to her, a handsome boy stood grinning at the girl. "Is that you and Mayor Hank?"

Gretel nodded. Without really meaning to, I leaned into her until our sides were touching. It's how I used to sit with Grandma. Gretel didn't seem to mind. She kept talking.

"Dad was so happy with the painting, he told Harold he only wished Sinkville drew in more customers to see it. 'Something like that needs to be seen, doesn't it?' Dad had said. Harold offered to call up his friends." She laughed again. "Dad didn't realize Harold meant the young people planning sit-ins, protests, and demonstrations! Our little diner soon became a hotspot for promoting the movement, with meetings held right here."

"Wow," Kerica whispered.

"These kids, they weren't used to being invited to a public place for meetings. Especially a restaurant in a mostly white town like Sinkville. They came in primed for a fight, so used to being turned away, threatened

113

with arrest, or generally mistreated wherever they went. But Dad just shook each person's hand and told them the day's specials. Harold even mentioned to Dad that one of the young men needed work." Gretel tilted her head toward the kitchen. I heard whistling and saw a blur of movement. "Chef Johnny's been with us ever since."

"Why isn't the painting in the window still there?" Kerica asked.

"A couple years ago, we had a bad storm. Used to be a tree growing in the parking lot. A branch went right through the window. By then, everyone knew all were welcomed here, so the painting wasn't necessary." Gretel paused, looking straight at Kerica. "But maybe we could use the reminder, even now. What are your painting skills like, Kerica? I can see you're an artist from your sketches there."

Kerica's cheeks flushed. "I'm okay, I guess."

I grabbed the placemat and held it closer to see what Kerica had been doodling. It was a drawing of me and Gretel, both of us midlaugh.

"I didn't know you could draw like this!" I said. "Why didn't you tell me you like art?"

Kerica shrugged. "It didn't come up."

"Well," Gretel said. "How about putting it to the test. Why don't you try re-creating the painting on paper for me? Then we can talk about commissioning you to re-create it on the window. I sort of miss it."

"Really?" Kerica asked. "I'd love that!"

Gretel patted Kerica's hand again, then gathered our menus in one arm. But she paused before getting up. She drummed her fingernails against the Formica top and sort of nodded to herself, like she was having a conversation in her head before speaking aloud. "Sinkville, it's not much of a town. It's got its problems just as sure as the Mill stinks. But it's a good town. One that'll break down barriers when it can. One that will focus on the sweet instead of the sour.

"And Harold?" She again turned and looked at the mayor. Sometimes you just know things. In that moment, I just knew that when she looked at Mayor Hank, she still saw the handsome, passionate boy he once was. "He's the one to credit for most of that."

Kerica must've seen it, too. "How long have you and Mayor Hank been girlfriend and boyfriend?"

Gretel brought the menus to her chest like a shield. She shook her head so hard her dangly earrings whipped her cheeks. "Ah, no. It's not like that. We're just friends. I haven't even had a boyfriend since I took over this place after Dad passed. And that was forty years ago!"

"Maybe it could be like that," I suggested. "Is there a Missus Mayor?"

Gretel laughed. "Nah, Harold's as married to this town as I am to this diner." She sighed and glanced toward the counter where Mayor Hank still sat. "I thought maybe, once . . . but, no. That passion of his is for our town. Not for me."

Kerica cocked an eyebrow at her. "You should ask him out."

Gretel giggled like she was our age. "I'm pushing seventy, sweet cheeks. Those days are gone."

"What days are gone?" Suddenly the man himself, Mayor Hank, stood behind Gretel.

Gretel's face flushed and her mouth popped open. Kerica to the rescue. "We were just talking about what life was like when you guys were kids," she said. "Life back in the sixties."

Mayor Hank rolled back on his heels as a smile stretched across his face. "Those were the days, weren't they, Gretel?"

"So what did you do then?" I asked. "Like for dates and stuff."

Mayor Hank's face flushed, too. "I didn't go on many dates."

"Too busy saving the town, even then," Gretel murmured as she strode back to the kitchen with our menus. Mayor Hank turned to watch her leave, and again I had a flash of knowledge. He loved her. And she loved him back.

"You had to have had at least one date," Kerica pushed.

Mayor Hank studied his shoes for a second. "I do remember a picnic by the Sycamore."

"What sycamore?" I asked.

Kerica sat with her arms folded and her eyes wide. She shook her head. To the mayor, she said, "Excuse my best friend. She doesn't get out much."

I crossed my arms and wiggled my eyebrows at her. "Blind and new, remember?"

Kerica nodded. "Forgot about the blind thing for a sec, sorry." She shifted in her seat, giving Tooter the leeway to put his paws on the table and lick the grease from the hamburger plate. Mayor Hank's eyes widened at the sight of a dog in the diner but he didn't say anything.

"What sycamore?" I asked louder. This whole everyone-knows-but-you-so-I'm-going-to-stretch-out-telling-you-as-long-as-possible thing was getting old.

"We've got to introduce this girl to the Sinkville Sycamore, Kerica," said Mayor Hank, laying down a few bills to cover our milkshakes. "Time for a field trip."

Chapter Nine

How had I not noticed the Sinkville Sycamore before? It was only a few blocks from the Williams Diner.

The Sycamore stretched so high that its top branches were blurs. Even Kerica said she had to squint to make out the delicate-looking bone-white tips of the branches. The trunk was mottled brown. An entire class of kindergarteners could stand, arms stretched out and fingertip to fingertip, and not enclose this tree.

Sinkville Sycamore stood sentinel in the center of a park, encircled by a ring of boulders. Barefoot children leaped from rock to rock, laughing and playing. Elderly men played chess at a bistro table. A woman held a crying baby to her chest on a bench nearby. The laughter, camaraderie, and life combined like a kaleidoscope as we approached the massive tree. But as we got closer, the noise muffled. I felt a silence unfold like new leaves.

The bark felt rough under my hands, but not like it'd splinter my fingers. More weathered, like skin about to peel after a sunburn. I could fit my hand in ridges of the tree. I had never climbed a tree before, but this one made me want to. Only there was no way I could jump to the closest branch, which stretched out like a tree of its own growing horizontally. It made a perfect bench, big enough for a picnic of twenty, before gently tilting toward the sun. At least thirty other limbs twisted and creaked above that bottom branch, each one looking wider than even my dad could encircle with his arms.

"How tall is it?" Kerica asked.

"Oh, I'd say a hundred feet at least," Mayor Hank answered. "And at least two centuries old."

We stared silently at the tree for a few more minutes. I pulled out my notebook and started to sketch the tree. My sketch didn't come close to capturing it, but I tried.

I want to say that the tree was beautiful. But it wasn't. It was hideous. Huge, massive, twisty, ugly. But somehow, that made it majestic. I thought about what it had blindly faced in two hundred years. Sure, it was rooted in the same spot, but how many storms had it weathered? How many times had lightning threatened one of its limbs? It had stayed still and stubborn through the rise of the town. It breathed in thousands of people's air, exhaling oxygen. How many lovebirds carved their names in its bark? Kerica counted a dozen aged hearts; certainly there were more that she couldn't see. How many fights had it heard? How many birds' nests had it cradled? How many dirty toes and fingers had scrambled up its sides? Even though it always stayed still, the tree never stopped changing. Its bark broke away to reveal smoother, paler bark below as it grew.

"Can I borrow a piece of paper?" Kerica asked.

I smiled, knowing her sketch would be so much cooler than mine. "Here," I said, and handed her my notebook and pencil. "No way I can draw this tree."

"You sure?" Kerica asked.

I nodded, and she stepped backward from the tree, settling on a bench a few yards away; I guess so she could see it better. I tried to lock the image of the tree in my mind instead. I didn't realize my eyes were closed until I felt Mayor Hank's breath on my head. I opened my eyes and saw that he was waiting for some kind of response from me. About the tree. Maybe about Sinkville. Maybe about me.

But then again, I thought, *maybe some people saw this and just thought,* wow, what a big tree. I tried to swallow down all the huge thoughts that shadowed my mind while standing under the Sycamore. Then I looked more closely at Mayor Hank and realized I didn't have to. He got it.

"It's amazing," I managed to mutter.

He smiled slowly, one of those smiles that you feel more than see.

Mayor Hank knelt in front of me, his hand buried in one of the tree's ridges. "This tree, it's been through so much. Right here in Sinkville. Who knows where these boulders came from, forming this perfect circle? A lot of folks say the first inhabitants here, the Native Americans, arranged them. This tree saw them leave. Then it stood here while the Civil War waged. Notices about runaway slaves used to be nailed to its trunk. The nails are still in the trunk. This tree was here through the Mill coming. It was here for every generation of Sinkville."

I wished for my notebook back as I let the idea of the tree seeing everything that happened in Sinkville wash over me. Just like I had tried to lock the image of the tree in my mind, I tried to capture Mayor Hank's words.

"Gretel, she loves this tree," he said softly. "I was a busboy for her daddy in high school. You should've seen her then. Prom Queen, cheerleader, debate captain. The most beautiful girl you'd ever seen."

"I can picture it," I said behind closed eyelids.

"She used to come here every day after school. Just sit under these branches and think." He shifted a little beside me, resting his head in one of the trunk's ridges. "She was surrounded by people all the time, friends and hangers-on. I knew she came here to be by herself. But I used to come anyway. I'd sit on one side of the trunk, she on the other."

"It's so big! You probably didn't even see each other."

Mayor Hank nodded. "Yes, that's how I justified it. But after a while, we'd somehow end up on the same side. And then we'd be beside each other. We wouldn't talk. Just sit beside each other."

I thought about that, how Kerica and I could spend all day sitting next to each other in the hand chairs, just reading and not talking but still feeling like we were there together. "That sounds nice."

But Mayor Hank shook his head, like he was scattering the memory. "It was nice. But it wasn't enough."

"What do you mean?"

"All my life, I've never had a problem telling folks what I think. But I could never work up the courage to tell Gretel that I was sweet on her. After about a month of us sitting side by side here, she said what she loved most about this tree was knowing that she wasn't the only one who fell in love in its shade. If that wasn't an invitation to speak up, I don't know what was. But my stupid mind just shut down. Couldn't speak."

"Did you tell her the next day?"

"I was going to. I planned to ask her to prom. I packed a picnic—cheese sandwiches and juice. I was going to tell her I loved her." He rubbed the heels of his hands into his eyes. "But Gretel wasn't sitting here."

I scooted a little closer to the mayor, but stayed silent. I wanted him to know I was listening but I didn't want him to be pushed out of his memory. "Then what happened?"

"I hardly think that's appropriate to share."

"She liked you, too. She told us you were handsome." His eyebrows shot up. "And passionate," I added.

Sure enough, he started talking again. "I found her at the diner, sharing a milkshake with the football star. I tried to tell her I liked her, but she said if I really cared, I wouldn't have waited until someone else asked her out."

Mayor Hank told me that after that, he did everything to impress her. "I even started a 'Save the Sycamore' campaign to turn this into a park, to make sure it never became fodder for the Mill or got torn down. Heck, I even became mayor to get her to notice me again. Sinkville's youngest mayor, not even out of college when I ran."

"And you're a fantastic mayor," I said. Even though he was actually the first mayor I had ever met. And so far, all I had seen him actually do was visit a tree and drink milkshakes. But still, he had my vote. If I could, you know, vote.

Mayor Hank grinned, and I caught a glimpse of the boy again. He stood up and held out a hand to help me up. "You know, it's pretty unprofessional of me, there. To share all that with you, especially since I heard you're entering the contest. I hope you won't make note of all that silly Gretel stuff."

I crossed my arms and knocked him with a glare. "Mayor Hank! There is nothing silly about love. But I won't write it down."

As Mayor Hank got up and strode away, I realized I hadn't smelled the Sinkville stink all day. "Mayor Hank!" I called to his back.

He turned, too far away for me to see his face. I rushed toward him. "You should tell her. Plan another picnic."

He flapped his hand in the air like he was pushing away a gnat. "Too much time has passed."

"She told us you don't back down from things you care about. If you still like her, you should tell her."

Kerica and Tooter wandered over as Mayor Hank left. She handed me the notebook, complete with an incredible sketch of the Sycamore. I quickly scribbled Mayor Hank's words on the next page.

"This tree," Kerica said, her eyes wrinkled, "it freaks me out. Did you know the Native Americans believed sycamores were cursed by evil spirits and that's why they're so twisted? That the trees suck up all that's wrong? I read about it."

"Of course you did," I laughed and patted the spot beside me where Mayor Hank had been a minute earlier. Tooter curled up on my lap. Kerica sat down next to me, eventually leaning against the trunk but without the ease that Mayor Hank had. Even though it was still steamy hot outside, the air was cooler under the tree and smelled fresh as laundry straight from the dryer.

I got sunscreen out of my bag and spread it on my arms and face. I fanned myself with my sunhat since we were in the shade. "I'm sorry I never thought about what you and Gretel were saying. About how things used to be. That must be hard to think about."

For a few seconds, I worried I had said something stupid. Kerica's arms crossed and she half-turned from me. Then she huffed out of her nose and sat back. "It's hard to think about how things were for my grandma. I mean, I can understand why she's so set in her ways, you know? So closed off."

I nodded.

"And things are so much better than they used to be. But they're still hard."

I put my arm around my friend. "Do you mean what you said earlier, about not fitting in?"

"Yeah." Kerica shrugged. "It's kind of tough to talk about."

126

"First rule about being best friends: we can talk about anything. Like the fact that you're an awesome artist. I didn't know about that, either."

"It's not artwork," Kerica said, her head drooping. "It's just doodling. It doesn't count."

I pulled out the paper placemat I had folded and slipped into my back pocket with the notebook. I smoothed it on my lap. "Sure it does," I said. "You just need someone to notice it. And soon the whole town will, too. Will you sign it for me?" I handed her my pen.

"Don't be stupid," Kerica laughed. "I'm not signing a placemat!"

"Well, don't think of it as an autograph. Just write your name and phone number on it. Now that we're officially best friends, we're going to need some non-library talk time."

"I'd like that," Kerica said. She wrote her number, and I promised to call her that night.

"I've been thinking," Kerica said after a long pause, "about your mom."

"What about her?" I asked, my heart thumping for some reason.

Kerica shifted. "I saw the books my mom was pulling for her at the library."

"About schools for the blind?" I snapped.

But Kerica shook her head, the beads in her braids clicking gently as she did. "No, not those." She peeled bark off a fallen twig. "About depression."

I bit my lip. I'm not sure why. It wasn't like I could say anything. In those two words, all that I had been feeling—being lost in other people's stories—was gone. Only my story was left, a story about a girl on her own because her mom was too sad to be a mom.

"I'm sorry," Kerica whispered, so softly I could barely hear her. This time, she was the one who shuffled closer to me. I let my head tilt so it fell against her shoulder.

"I just wish I could talk to her," I said. And that my chin wasn't so wobbly.

"Maybe she needs to be the one to talk first."

Mrs. Morris and Kerica gave me a ride home that afternoon. James wasn't home and Mom was resting. So I repeated in my head, *Advocate for myself!* and tackled the laundry. Mom used to stack our clean clothes in piles according to the drawers they went into. All the socks and undies on top, then pj's, then shirts, then shorts, so we could just grab a stack and put them away. But some other people in this house could learn to advocate for themselves, it seemed. I stacked the clothes according to how I pulled them out of the basket. They were wrinkly from being in the basket too long, and I'm not so great at folding. I just sort of folded the T-shirts over and rolled the socks into balls.

"When did you start doing the laundry?" James grumbled when he got home a few minutes later.

"I put a load in this morning. Out of underwear again," I shrugged, acting like me doing laundry wasn't a huge deal when it *totally* was.

I pushed his stack of clothes on the coffee table toward him.

When he came back into the living room, he had a dust rag and some spray.

"Can't let you have all the fun," he said. "Pretty soon even you're going to see the dust."

I laughed and threw a sock at his head but of course he batted it out of the air. Next thing I knew, my head was covered by a shirt he had snatched from the basket. I pretended I was about to spray him with dust spray, and he tackled me. Tooter jumped on top of James and snarled, making both of us stop for a second. Then the dumb dog twirled in circles, like twenty times. All those clean clothes flew everywhere, but we were laughing too hard to care.

Both of us were smiling as we picked up the clothes and refolded them. That is, until James spotted Mom standing in the doorway. His smile vanished, his arms stiffened, and he shuttered up again.

Mom gave me a small smile and then headed back to her room.

A little later, when James's bedroom door slammed shut and the house became too quiet, I went into Mom's room. There was a medicine bottle on her nightstand with a glass of water beside it. Light seeped in through the cracks in the mini blinds. Mom was covered with blankets, a mound on the left side of the bed.

I crept into her bed, curling against her back and wrapping my arm around her. For a long time, she didn't move. But after a while, she rolled so we faced each other. She pulled the blankets up over me, too.

I was still snoozing, somewhere between being awake and being asleep, when I realized Mom was talking to me in a hushed, whispery voice, " . . . doctor's a couple weeks ago. I got some medicine. It should start working in a week or two. I'm already feeling a little better . . ."

I burrowed closer to Mom, snuggling my head between her face and shoulder.

"I've been blue before, but never this long. I'm so sorry, sweetie. I love you. I love you."

"I love you, too," I whispered back, or maybe I just thought it as I fell back asleep.

When Dad came in and flipped on the lights, I couldn't believe a whole hour had passed. Was this the way it was for Mom all day? Time passing by while her eyes were closed. I thought she'd be grouchy; she never had liked waking up. But she pulled me closer and squeezed. I knew she was smiling, even though I couldn't see her face.

"Hey, sleepyheads!" Dad chirped. "Anyone want some dinner?"

We went to the Williams Diner even though it was a Tuesday and we never went out to dinner on a Tuesday. "Twice in one day!" Gretel said as I walked in. I just grinned as Dad's face flushed. Guess he thought she was talking about him.

Mom and James stood transfixed at the door. "I know," I whispered to them. "Sounds just like Grandma, doesn't she?" They glanced at each other with wide eyes. They looked so much alike, I had to smile. I led them to the booth. "Miss Gretel, I think my mom could use a PB&J shake. Extra coconut."

"Coming right up, Alice!"

Soon I was sipping my second shake of the day, thinking life in Sinkville wasn't too bad after all.

And then Sandi came into the diner.

Chapter Ten

For a while after I was born, Mom became a freelance writer. She traded journeying around the world with an internationally famous magazine for assignments from the local newspaper. At first, Mom hired babysitters and worked like she always had—interviewing her subjects face-to-face. But the salary was terrible and after paying the sitter, there was little left. So she did phone interviews instead, planning them around my naps and James's TV time.

One day, Mom was interviewing a surgeon about a new technique in cardiac medicine. The interview was not going well. Mom had figured the phone interview would last about a half-hour, just long enough to describe the new method, but instead the surgeon had spent that amount of time and longer asking Mom questions about her background, her experience in journalism, and her methods of ensuring she was getting correct information from her sources before it was printed.

Mom knew she had to wind up the interview quickly as James began slamming toy trucks together at her feet. She frantically waved her hands in front of her and shook her head as James stood and came closer with a big grin on his slobbery face. The surgeon heard the clicking of the laptop keys suddenly stop and said, "Can you repeat back to me what I just said?"

"Um, let me check," Mom murmured.

And that was when little James very politely, very courteously leaned into the phone and said, "In a moment, I'm going to need you to wipe my butt."

The surgeon hung up.

That was the last day Mom wrote for a newspaper or a magazine. She used to keep journals for us, but she stopped writing in those, too.

Before Sandi and her mom came into Williams Diner, I thought about that. Maybe what Mom needed wasn't a job like the work-from-home and cafeteria chef positions I had circled in that newspaper.

Maybe she needed to find stories and write.

"There she is!" Sandi shouted and pointed to me. "She's the one whose dog assaulted me!"

James spit a mouthful of shake out onto the table as Mom and Dad gasped. "Is she talking about Tooter?" he laughed.

I felt blood rush to my face, making me feel like I was boiling from the inside out as every face in the diner turned to look at me. "It wasn't an *assault*," I said. "It was just a little peeing and growling."

Sandi yanked her mom's arm toward us. She was maybe a half-foot taller than Sandi, with the same bright blonde hair. Only where Sandi's was pulled back into a smooth ponytail, her mom's was in a tightly twisted bun. She wore a white suit with navy trim and it fit her perfectly. I had a feeling that's not the type of thing you could buy off a rack at the department store.

"I understand that we have a situation," she said in clipped tones.

"I'm not sure *I* understand," Dad replied. He half-stood in the booth and put out his hand. "I'm Ted Confrey, and this is my wife, Dana."

Sandi's mom stared at Dad's outstretched hand for a few uncomfortable seconds before taking it in her own. "Elizabeth McAllister."

"Please, have a seat and bring us up to speed." Mom gestured to the table next to our booth but Mrs.

McAllister didn't make a move to sit down. Just slightly behind her, Sandi crossed her arms and glared at me. She crossed her legs, I'm sure just so we could see the large Band-Aid across her shin.

"What is going on?" James snapped.

Elizabeth McAllister's chin bopped into the air as she stared down at us, like the very sight of our family disgusted her. "What's going on is that earlier today I was interrupted during a very important business meeting by my traumatized daughter."

All of our heads—and I mean everyone's head in the entire diner—swiveled to look toward Sandi, who looked triumphant, not traumatized.

"I'm sorry to hear that," Dad said, obviously confused. "But I'm still not sure what that has to do with us or Tooter."

"Tooter?" Mrs. McAllister snipped. "That's what you call the beast that attacked my daughter?"

"There's that word again. Attacked. Could you maybe expand on that a bit?" Uh-oh. Mom was getting mad. Her own chin tilted sky high.

"He peed on me!" Sandi burst in, pointing to her leg. "And growled at me!"

Again, James spit milkshake across the table. Across the diner, patrons half-coughed, half-laughed into paper napkins.

Elizabeth McAllister turned back to us and pointed at Sandi's bandaged leg. "The *dog* also scratched her leg. It left a mark."

"Every scratch leaves a mark." There I go with the mouth diarrhea again. Dad stared at me with his mouth hanging open and James bumped my foot under the table. "He was just putting his paw back down," I said a little softer.

Elizabeth McAllister crossed her slender arms and glared down at us all. I squirmed in my seat.

"Alice," Dad said in his extra stern Dad-voice, "what do you have to say about this?"

I peeked through my lashes at Mom, who seemed to be keeping her mouth closed with a lot of effort. "Um," I muttered, "Sandi was laying on the grass, so maybe Tooter was just confused . . ."

"Yeah, right!" Sandi snapped. "I think Seeing Eye dogs can *see* the difference between a lawn and *someone's body!*"

Again people chuckled into napkins around the diner. James ducked so hair covered his face as Mom and Dad said, "Seeing Eye dog?" at the same time.

"You thought," Dad half-laughed, "Tooter is a service animal? Hardly!"

Again everyone swiveled toward me. "Well, he does sort of help me . . ."

Mom's voice was quiet, which made it even scarier than Dad's booming voice. "Where exactly has Tooter been?"

"Just the library," I said. "And the diner. We went to the lake, too, but Mr. Hamlin was okay with that."

"Did you know about this?" Dad asked Mom.

She shook her head. Dad's eyes narrowed at her.

Elizabeth McAllister's already glaring eyes narrowed even further. I swear, it was like an unplanned staring contest. "So, you mean to say that not only is this animal assaulting my child, it's masquerading as a service animal?" She turned and glanced behind her at Sandi, who was standing in the same crossed-arms, snooty-central stance. "I've lost my appetite."

"But!" Sandi chirped, her arms dropping and voice whining. "I wanted a milkshake. You promised!"

"Hang on," Dad said. "I'm sure we can resolve this."

"We have nothing to resolve." Elizabeth McAllister turned her back to us. "You'll be hearing from my lawyer."

"What about the milkshakes?" Sandi stomped behind her mom out of the diner.

No one talked the rest of dinner. Even Gretel just handed us our check without her usual chitchat. By the time we got home, the silence felt thicker than a wet comforter. Mom got out of the car, walked into the house, and went straight to bed. She didn't even turn on the light in her room. Dad went to his office and closed the door. It was just James and me in the living room. And Tooter, of course. He tried to break up the tension by dragging his hind legs across the carpet and then letting out a long, loud fart.

James sunk into the couch and put his feet up on the coffee table.

"Are you mad at me?" I whispered.

"A little bit." James shifted on the couch, rooting through the cushions for the remote. He found it, turned on the TV, and patted the seat next to him for Tooter. The dumb dog tried twice to jump up on the couch and missed both times. James bent down and scooped him up with a sigh. "But it's not your fault. It just sucks. Mom was actually starting to look a little better."

I hung my head. "I know. Now things are going to get even worse."

"Maybe," James shrugged. "Or maybe they'll just change."

"Speaking of change, have you noticed how different Tooter is lately?"

"You mean the way he pees on people?" James laughed.

"Not just that, like the growling, the way he drags his legs, and the way he can't jump."

James ruffled Tooter's fur on top of his head. Tooter rolled onto his back for belly rubs. "He's old, Alice. Older than you."

I sat down next to him and Tooter. "Do you think they'll take Tooter away?"

"Nah." James rubbed Tooter's belly. The dog growled softly under his breath, flipped over, turned in a circle, farted, and sat back down.

I squirmed in my seat, feeling the reporter's notebook in my back pocket dig into my hip. "Do you still hate it here?"

James shrugged and flipped through the channels. "It's not all bad."

"Because of *Sarah*." I drug out her name like a song note.

"Shut up." But I could see James's lips twitch.

"You like here. Admit it."

He sighed and crossed his arms. "I don't hate it anymore."

"Knew it."

James elbowed me in the side. "Don't sweat the thing with Tooter. No one's actually going to go after a dumb old dog for peeing on them. Sandi's mom is just pissed. She'll get over it."

I smiled, and it felt like breaking through concrete; my whole body turned from rock to liquid there on the couch next to my brother. And I knew it wasn't just my worry about Tooter that melted. For the first time in a long time, I thought maybe we'd all be okay.

I pulled out my notebook and scribbled a few more notes about the Sycamore, Mayor Hank, Gretel, and Mr. Hamlin.

"No way." Mom stood with her arms crossed in the kitchen, shaking her head at me and Tooter.

"But Mom!" I whined. "I need to find out more about town!"

"There is absolutely no way in the world I'm going to let you take Tooter out of this house. He's grounded until this Sandi thing blows over."

"Can I go by myself then?"

Mom tilted her head at me and stared me down, like I was a tomato she was checking for dents and bruises before putting in the grocery cart. "I'm not comfortable with that," she said after a long pause.

"Well, what am I supposed to do then?" I crossed my arms, too, and sized her up the same way she had me. She usually was still sleeping when Tooter and I left for the library. But here she was, up and dressed. She almost looked like Seattle Mom, who, by the time

I got up in the morning, already had exercised, drank a couple cups of coffee, and was clapping her hands to get us moving. Only this Mom didn't remember to brush her hair and clearly could use another cup—or pot—of coffee.

Mom must've noticed me taking in her frizzy cotton candy hair because she ran her fingers through it a couple times while making *hmm*ing sounds like she was trying to figure out an answer to my question. To me, the answer was obvious: Let me go to the library.

Poor Tooter! He seemed so confused about whether we were going or not that he just kept trotting around the kitchen island in sad little circles. After about the twentieth rotation, I snapped, "Go lay down!" But he kept going, so I turned my back to him.

I pulled out my folded cane from my backpack. "I can manage by myself," I said to Mom. Okay, I sort of snapped instead of said.

Mom's hands stilled mid–hair combing. "You've been using your cane?" she asked. She knelt down so her face was just a few inches from mine and touched the white cane like it was a long-forgotten friend come to visit. A little reluctantly, I remembered how much she used to plead with me to use the cane and venture out a little more on my own when we lived in Seattle. I never had, though. I always had Eliza or another friend to go with me.

"Yeah." I shrugged but my mouth was having a hard time not breaking into a proud smile as Mom nodded with approval. Her own mouth seemed to be struggling with something, too. It kept forming silent words and stopping.

Finally, she settled on, "Why do you need to go to the library so badly?"

I pulled out my reporter's notebook from my still-open backpack. "I need to pull together all my notes and start writing my Sinkville Success Stories essay."

Mom's eyebrow arched. Okay, time for another confession. Strictly speaking, it wasn't *my* reporter's notebook. Remember that I found a stack of them in one of the unpacked boxes? I figured Mom wouldn't mind since they weren't being used, but I never actually asked her permission. She bit her lip but didn't say anything about it.

"Well, I don't see why you need to go to the library for that." Mom walked over to the kitchen table, which was covered with half-folded laundry, some unopened mail, and a couple dirty breakfast dishes. She stretched out her arm and swiped all of it into the laundry basket on the floor. "We can tackle it right here."

My mind snagged for a second on *we.* I had been doing so much on my own lately. But I dumped the backpack on the floor and took a seat at the table. I texted Kerica that it didn't look like I'd be coming in that morning. Mom sighed, but not her usual I'm-so-tired-and-going-back-to-bed sigh. This was more of a thank-you sigh, if that makes any sense. I squeezed her hand when she sat down next to me and searched her face. For some reason, her eyes filled with tears, even though she was smiling and I really thought she was feeling happy instead of sad. "I'm sor—"

But I cut her off before she could finish apologizing. "I've got a bunch of success stories, but I also have this tree story and I can't figure out how to pull it all together."

Mom's eyes dried as I told her my stories. After just about a half-hour of talking in circles—but now eating peanut butter by the spoonful while at it—Mom suddenly said, "Stop!"

"What?" My heart hammered. Did she think this was stupid? That I didn't have a chance?

"I think we need to take a field trip." She grinned and pulled her hair back with an elastic band. "Let's go, Alice. Show me around Sinkville."

Chapter Eleven

Before we left, Mom grabbed her camera bag. She never was famous for her photography, but she had an awesome camera. A photographer she used to travel with sold her the camera when he upgraded to a newer model. It's the kind that has a huge telescopic lens. Seeing it, I had this weird déjà vu moment where I heard the fluttering of quick clicks as I toddled around our old kitchen.

Mom pulled the camera out of the bag and wiped off some of the dust with an old towel. She held the camera up to her eye and clicked a few times, then aimed it at me. "Smile, Sunshine!" She pressed the button a few times. "We need some images of the reporter in action."

She was the one smiling as we stepped outside, pulling sunhats onto our heads, but it quickly turned into a grimace. "Ugh! That smell! It hits me every time we leave the house."

"What smell?" I asked, clicking the cane down the sidewalk toward the lake.

Just like I had hoped, Mr. Hamlin was sitting on the dock whittling as we approached. "Hey there, Gnome Girl," he drawled as I skipped up the wooden planks toward him.

"Alice! Be careful!" Mom shouted. The planks were a little crooked, and I guess skipping up or down them when your eyes move back and forth all the time and you aren't exactly a good swimmer isn't the brightest thing in the world to do, but I was having a skippy sort of day.

"Ah, you've brought a friend today," said Mr. Hamlin, rising slowly out of his lawn chair.

He and Mom shook hands and introduced themselves like adults while I picked up the work-in-progress from Mr. Hamlin's chair. It looked pretty much like a picked over piece of wood. Little chunks were missing from a couple sides and he had cut it so it was more like a triangle than a square.

"What's it going to be?" I asked as he finally settled back into his creaky chair.

"Not sure yet," he answered. "Fingers haven't decided."

I handed it to him and he went back to work, pecking away at the wood. It made a steady scraping sound.

Combined with the laps of water against the dock, it made sad background music as I told Mom the story of Mr. Hamlin's drowned house. Mom, who had been snapping shots of the lake, turned her camera toward Mr. Hamlin as I got to the part about Sarah wanting to be a farmer and how she was going to college next year even though she was only a year older than James.

I didn't have to see to know that Mr. Hamlin was smiling. I could tell by how Mom leaned in and clicked the shutter a bunch more times. She handed me the camera and I squinted into the little square display of the picture. I had to hold it about a half-inch from my eye and shade it with my hands, but I could see the soft little grin on Mr. Hamlin's weathered face.

"Well, we've got more of Sinkville to check out," I told Mr. Hamlin a few minutes later. He nodded and sort of grunted but didn't look up from the piece of wood.

I heard him mutter, "Come on now, whatcha gonna be?" to the wood as we walked back across the dock toward land.

"That was kind of a sad story," Mom murmured. She twisted her neck back and forth like she was shaking off muscle pain. I sighed through my nose. Here's where it was going to end, this little glimpse of my old mom. Here's where she'd tell me she was tired and we needed to go home. Stupid, stupid, stupid of me to start off with a flooded house story. I felt like slapping myself on the forehead. She was depressed! *Depressed.* And the first day she was ready to see Sinkville, I tell her all about a man watching his house drown.

Sure, I focused on how it led to Mr. Hamlin's son going to college and how proud he was about that. But Mom would focus on the sad part, I just knew it.

"All right," Mom said with a sigh. Here would come the "let's go home." But instead she said, "Where to now?"

"You mean it?" I squealed. Like, seriously squealed. It was as if she asked me if I wanted a chocolate bar or a new puppy.

Mom laughed. "You tell me, kiddo." She adjusted the camera strap around her neck. "This is your project. I'm game to keep going if you are."

I started to say, "Are you sure?" but bit it back. I thought for a second instead. I wanted part of my essay to focus on how Mayor Hank supported civil rights through the Williams Diner. Both he and Gretel would be found at the diner, but given that it was where Sandi and her mom had been such jerks to us the night before, it probably wouldn't be the best place to go. I was kind of toying around with making Mr. Hamlin's granddaughter a story all of its own—the way she benefited from the lake but wants to go back to farming—but I figured wherever we found Sarah, we'd find James . . . and James probably didn't want his mom to show up wherever his crush was. So that left one place. The Sycamore.

I squinted at Mom, who was pulling some spray sunscreen out of her bag and shaking it, getting ready to squirt it all over my arms. This was a very, very Mom thing to do. As in, regular Mom. Seattle Mom.

"The Sycamore," I said.

"The sycamore," Mom repeated. She didn't say it with a capital "S," I could tell. But I knew she would soon.

We stopped by the library to use the restroom and to renew Mom's books, and, of course, say hi to Kerica and Mrs. Morris. While there, Mom asked for the quickest way to get to the Sinkville Sycamore. Mrs. Dexter, in her cloud of lavender, didn't shout the directions out as loudly as she would've if it were just me. But she did cross her arms and glare down her long, shiny nose at me.

"One more thing," she said as we turned to go. "I've heard that . . . that . . . *dog* of yours is just a regular dog."

Mom's cheeks flushed. "Yes, I'm sorry about that. If I had any idea that was happening, I would've—"

With a wave of her arm and another punch of lavender in the face, Mrs. Dexter broke in, "I just want to know one thing."

Mom and I tilted our heads toward her in unison.

"How did it know what I was saying? I told it where the children's section is, how to get to the lake, and so on. And it listened! The blind girl here, she got to those places!"

Mom's mouth twitched as she turned toward me and back to Mrs. Dexter. "The blind girl here? Her name is Alice. And she can *hear.*" Mom leaned against the reference desk toward Mrs. Dexter like she was sharing a secret. "Alice's eyes might work differently than yours, but she is just as intelligent as someone with 20/20 vision. Maybe even smarter than some. Have a nice day, Mrs. Dexter."

Mom was practically bouncing as we left the library, although the Mill stink made her crinkle her nose. She squished up her face a little at the smell then grinned at me. "Was that woman like that every time you came to the library?"

I nodded.

She snorted. "I hope you didn't let it bother you."

I shook my head. "Nah."

"Good," Mom said. "So what's so special about this tree?"

I told Mom all about Mayor Hank saving the tree to impress Gretel as we made our way toward the Sycamore. I could tell we were getting close when Mom adjusted the camera and started clicking away.

By now we were crossing the circle of boulders. The tree's twisted limbs scratched at the sky. It seemed even bigger than the first time I'd seen it.

"This is the Sycamore?" Mom murmured. I didn't answer. I didn't have to. She went around the tree, snapping shot after shot. I settled down at the trunk and pulled out my notes, adding details from our day, like Mr. Hamlin's soft grin and just how green the grass around the tree grew.

It took me awhile to realize the clicking camera was much closer. Mom was taking shots of me sitting under the tree. After a few minutes, she moved to sit beside me.

We didn't say anything to each other for a long time. I mean, a really long time. Like the sun dipped lower in the sky and the clouds purpled. Everything I was carrying with me—all my worries and responsibilities and frights—suddenly trickled down from my shoulders onto my lap. I was so focused on myself—on this project, on what was going to happen to Tooter, on where I was going to go to school next month—that it took me way too long to realize the same thing must've happened to Mom. Because she was crying.

Not sobbing cries like the ones I sometimes had heard from behind her closed doors shortly after we moved to Sinkville. But quiet, steady cries. Her tears slid down her cheeks like the waves on the lake. Just like the lake, they shouldn't have been there. But they were.

"Mom," I finally whispered, my voice softer than the breeze around us. "When are you going to be okay?"

Mom just tilted her head onto my shoulder, the way I had done with Kerica a day earlier. "I'm trying, Sunshine. I'm really trying."

"I'm sorry I brought you here," I said as those worries clawed back up to my shoulders.

"No, no," Mom said, slipping her arm around me and giving me a squeeze. It was like she knew what was happening and was blocking the worries. "No, darling. I'm glad I'm here. This tree. It's magical, isn't it?" She turned a little and ran her fingers along the bark between us. "It looks like it's inside-out. I think it turned me inside-out, too."

I squeezed the fingers of the hand still wrapped around me, then scribbled INSIDE-OUT TREE in my notepad.

"Want to go home?" I asked as her cheeks dried.

"Sure," Mom said. "But first, let me tell you I'm proud of you, Sunshine. You really did what I couldn't. You put yourself out there, made new friends, made a new—"

"Home," I finished for her, but quietly. I waited a couple seconds and held up the reporter's notebook. "Mom, there are a lot of other notebooks in that box outside your bedroom. If you wanted to write a little . . ."

Mom grabbed my notebook, flipping through the pages. "What would I write about?"

I shrugged. "You used to say everyone had a story. You could write yours."

Mom handed me back the notebook. She sighed quickly and slapped her hands against her legs, like she was pushing down a thought. When she spoke next, her voice was different deliberately happy and louder. "When is it due, anyway?"

"What?" I asked.

"The Sinkville Success Stories!" Mom laughed, less forced than before. "When is it due?"

I shrugged. "You know, I never really checked." I pulled the flyer out of my notebook. "Oh man! It's due in two weeks!"

"Better get started on the writing part," Mom smiled and pulled me closer before standing up. "Race you to the boulders?"

Then the cheater took off! I scrambled after her, knowing she'd let me catch up.

Just as we were leaving the park, I saw Mayor Hank. He was walking toward the tree with a basket under one arm. The other arm was around Gretel.

Chapter Twelve

*B*y *the time* we reached our block, Seattle Mom was fading fast. I could see it happen, the same way I could see when James tightened up and curled over as he got closer to the house on the days I was out with him. Only Mom didn't go into herself. She just sort of faded away. First her smile wasn't as bright. Then it wasn't there at all. Her footsteps went from brisk and steady to soft and slow. Her grip on my hand loosened until I was clasping just her fingertips.

"Are you tired?" I asked.

Mom smiled, but I could tell she had to work to do it. She nodded. "This . . . this thing I'm dealing with . . ."

"Depression?"

She startled at the word, her eyes cutting over to mine. "Yes. This depression. It takes some time. I think I've kicked it, but then . . ."

I squeezed her fingertips again. "We're almost home. I'll make dinner," I suggested.

Mom nodded, but I don't think she was really listening. I don't mean to brag, but I make a mean cup of chicken noodle soup. Open the can myself and everything. Chicken noodle soup and buttered bread for dinner.

Once we were home, Mom went straight to bed and I pulled the ingredients out of the pantry. Well, the ingredient, that is.

I was stirring the soupy globs apart and adding a can of water to the saucepan when James rushed through the kitchen door, skateboard kicked up into his hand and yelling Tooter's name.

"What's going on?" I asked. Mom's bedroom door opened and she rushed out, Tooter running at her heels.

"James?" she asked.

But James still looked panicked. His eyes wide, he knelt and picked up Tooter, who licked at his ears. "We've got to hide Tooter! They're going to be here soon!"

"Who?" Mom and I asked at the same time.

"The animal control people! They're coming for him!"

The doorbell rang just as my heart exploded in my chest.

James had been shadowing Sarah around Sinkville Animal Rescue when the veterinarian, Dr. Ross, told

Sarah to prep the quarantine area for a potentially dangerous dog.

"This happens sometimes," Sarah told James as she lined a cage with a fleece blanket and filled a water bottle. "When someone reports they've been assaulted by a dog, animal control workers go collect it and it's quarantined here for ten days while the doc looks for signs of aggression or rabies."

Dr. Ross snorted. "Don't know how aggressive this dog is going to be, with a name like Tooter."

After that, James took off for home.

Mom let the animal control workers into the house and I saw them smirk when they saw Tooter still licking at James's sweaty ears.

"This really isn't necessary," Mom told the two workers.

One of them, a woman, went up to Tooter and rubbed at his ears. "I'm sorry, ma'am. The dog has to come with us. Dr. Ross will take good care of him at the shelter."

Tooter twirled around twice in the transport cage and lay down. He panted, his stupid goofy face almost smiling like he was going on an adventure. I didn't realize I was crying until the tears dripped from my cheeks onto my neck. James moved closer to me, his shoulder brushing mine. When I looked at him, I gasped. His eyes were wide with fear, his face white. I was about to say, "Hey, take it easy! Look at Tooter, he's fine!" but James wasn't staring at Tooter with panic. He was watching Mom, waiting for her to crumble.

But Mom wasn't crumbling. She was fierce. Mom kept arguing with the workers, promising that we'd keep the dog inside, that this was a big misunderstanding, that they should at least wait until her husband came home. The two workers just nodded and kept securing the locks on the cage. They lifted it and Tooter let out a loud toot.

The next morning, we were waiting at Sinkville Animal Rescue when the doors opened. Mom stood just behind me and James.

"You didn't have to come, Mom." James's hair was loose over his forehead as always and Mom lightly pushed it back with her fingertips. James flinched like her touch was a flame. Mom's fingers stilled and lowered limply.

I whapped James with my hip. What was he thinking? He nudged me back with his bony hip and gave me a "what?" look. But I could tell he felt bad, too. For some reason, it made me think of when Mom had said "we" yesterday when she was talking about my project. How it had made me angry for a second, the way she wanted to pick up right where she had been as if weeks of her being part zombie hadn't happened.

Maybe that's what James was feeling now. I tried to give him an I-get-it-but-you-got-to-give-her-a-chance look, but let's face it. I'm not that talented facially. Blame the eyes, I guess. He looked totally confused. "Are you feeling sick?" he asked.

Mom whipped around to me. "Oh, honey!" She put her hand in mine. "I'm sure Tooter is fine."

When the heavy doors pulled back, there stood Sarah. Behind me, James sucked in his breath. Sarah's eyes locked with his, and I swear I could feel vibrations of energy between the two of them.

Mom could, too, because I felt the whoosh of her hair as her head whipped between them. "I—I . . ." her voice trailed off. "I can only deal with one thing at time," she muttered.

"You're just in time!" Sarah clapped her hands together.

"Is something wrong? Did something happen to Tooter?" But I knew even as I asked that the dumb dog was fine. Sarah wasn't worried; she was super excited.

"I'm fine! We're all fine! You won't believe what we found today!" Sarah grabbed James by the arm and yanked him along the corridor. Mom and I glanced at each other and then trotted behind them.

159

When we reached the little room that Sarah had pulled James into, I still didn't know what was going on. They stood with Dr. Ross around a little table, peering in at something locked in a small cage. "Can you believe it?" Sarah asked. "I mean, they've got to be super rare."

"They are," Dr. Ross agreed. "Especially rare to find one this old. Most of the time, they die in infancy."

"Why? I mean, so what that it looks different." James's voice was strangely husky. He turned away from the cage. In two steps, he was at my side, turning me away from the table. "Let's get Tooter," he muttered.

But Sarah had turned toward Mom and me and I was close enough to see her wide eyes and the way the excitement on her face twisted into something else. I shimmied out of James's grip and moved toward the cage.

Dr. Ross continued, "They're not suited to living unprotected on their own. They can't blend in for obvious reasons. Their appearance makes them an ideal target for predators, plus their compromised vision puts them at an incredible disadvantage. It's amazing that it survived this long. These kinds of mutations almost never make it."

By then, of course, I knew. Whatever was locked in this cage was an albino.

An albino squirrel.

Mom's hands were steady on my shoulders. She squeezed gently. "It's beautiful."

Dr. Ross coughed slightly. "Yes, um. It is." I wasn't looking at him, just the squirrel, milky white and red-eyed, but I heard the doctor shift across the room. I felt his eyes on me, and I knew they were raking down from my paper white hair, my translucent skin, my darting eyes. "I didn't mean to offend. And I'm sorry if I did."

"No need to apologize," Mom said. "Right, Alice?"

"What happened to it?" I asked instead of answering Mom.

"Well, he fell." Dr. Ross leaned down on his elbows so our eyes were level though he was on the other side of the cage. "That's our best guess, anyway. The resident who called found him under a tree, apparently stunned."

"Squirrels can fall out of trees?" James asked. "Aren't they, like, tree ninjas, jumping all over the place?"

Dr. Ross nodded, but his eyes stayed locked on mine. "This squirrel doesn't have pigment in his eyes. He can't see as well and the sunshine likely hurts him since he has no protection from the glare. It leads to falls."

"Is he . . ." Mom left the rest of the question unspoken but I knew what she was asking. So did Dr. Ross.

"Yes, he's going to be fine. Nothing broken. I think he was just stunned. Didn't even put up a fight when I brought him here."

The squirrel was shaking in his cage, curled up in a corner. When I ran my finger along a bar of the enclosure, he squealed.

"I'm sorry!" I whispered to him. "Why didn't you let him go?" I have to admit, I was a little surprised at how angry my voice sounded. I didn't even realize I was mad until I had said it, but suddenly I was seething. So what if the squirrel fell? I'm sure that kind of stuff happens all the time. Why not just let him scamper off with his little squirrel friends?

Dr. Ross didn't answer for a long minute. When he did, he sounded so gentle that I had to look at him. His brown eyes stared steadily into mine and I knew he was going to tell me the truth. "It's a miracle he made it as long as he did. This is the safest place for him. We can learn about him and, at the same time, keep him safe.

"But you're not here about the squirrel, I presume." Dr. Ross stood up. "You're here to check on Tooter."

Tooter was in a large enclosure, his tail thumping like it does when he's happy. James and Sarah talked to him through the bars. When Mom, Dr. Ross, and I approached, he rolled onto his back. Kind of like, "Hey, while you're here, I could use a belly rub."

Behind me, Dr. Ross was telling Mom about quarantine. How it's a way to ensure that animals aren't aggressive or showing other signs of rabies. That it's standard procedure when there is a complaint about an attack.

James snorted.

"I understand there is some disagreement about whether this was an attack at all." Dr. Ross glanced at Sarah who nodded back to him.

"He peed on Sandi McAllister and she totally deserved it." I crossed my arms and glared up at the doctor, daring him to disagree.

But he didn't. He smiled. "I've met Elizabeth McAllister and Sandi," he said. "Tooter sure knows how to pick his targets."

"Tooter's foot came down on the girl's leg," Mom said, sounding annoyed. "It's been a while since we've had him groomed, so his claws are a little long, but I can't imagine the so-called injury is all that serious."

Dr. Ross nodded but didn't say anything. I guess Tooter did look a little shaggy, now that Mom had mentioned it.

"The point is, I don't see why we can't monitor him at home," Mom continued.

"I don't either," Dr. Ross said. "In fact, I was going to suggest it. We might catch some flak about it from the McAllisters, but it's pretty typical to give owners that option. We just need to be able to swing by and check on him at least once a day."

"Yes!" I flung into Dr. Ross's arms, which he apparently didn't expect because he tumbled backward, catching himself before we both fell.

"I take it that's the course you'd like to go with," he said as he straightened himself and me.

"Yes, I believe so," Mom laughed.

Mom and Dr. Ross talked about the quarantine rules and completed paperwork while James followed Sarah around the room, making sure the center's snakes, frogs, and turtles had enough water, the right temperature in their enclosures, and a snack or two. Most of them were formerly pets, Sarah explained. People didn't realize turtles would be around for fifty years when they bought them, so they'd drop them off at the center when they were tired of them. People hated stocking the freezer with dead rats for snakes. The frogs weren't native to the area and so had to be kept at the rescue permanently.

It all seemed sad to me, these abandoned critters. I let James and Sarah move on while I watched the frogs and turtles, wondering if they missed their owners.

Or were they glad they had moved here, where they were being taken care of and studied? A dark blue frog stared at me from the back of his aquarium. I watched a turtle stretch out his neck, nab a piece of shredded lettuce, and let his neck droop back as he nibbled. When I glanced back at the blue frog, it was in the middle of his cage, still staring at me. I moved toward the opposite side, where a snake twirled around a twig in his cage. I wondered if the frog liked living next door to something that likely wanted to eat him. When I turned back to the frog, I gasped. It was right up against the glass.

I probably could've continued the staring contest with the blue frog all day but Sarah's laughter broke my concentration. "Are you sure that's safe?" James asked. And that was all the invitation I needed to get closer. There was Sarah with about six fuzzy, long-tailed, and white-faced creatures scampering all up her shoulders and chest.

"Are those mini monkeys?" I asked.

Sarah laughed again, grabbing one of the furry lumps from the edge of her shoulder and placing it on her chest. "They're baby opossums. The mom was killed by a car but the babies survived. They're like kangaroos, carrying their babies in a pouch for a few weeks. Dr. Ross has been taking care of them, getting them ready to live on their own."

"They are so creepy," James said, extending a finger toward one of the babies. It bared its mini dagger teeth and hissed. Believe me, if I had been Sarah, there would've been opossum babies flung all over the place after that. But she just laughed, plucking the babies off and putting them back in the cage.

They moved on to feed some animals in the next room. I stayed by the baby opossums. Poor things. There they were, feeling safe as could be in their mama's pouch when *bam*! The accident happened and everything changed.

For some reason, it made me think of that poor scared squirrel.

James and Sarah didn't notice me leave the room. Dr. Ross and Mom were still talking in his office. Tooter didn't even look up as I passed his enclosure.

The squirrel stayed huddled in the corner of his cage, his red eyes watching me unblinkingly. I linked my fingers in the bars, and he squeaked. It was a high-pitched whistling sound. I thought at first it was a warning, but when I lifted the barred part of the cage to fit my hand underneath it, he didn't move away from my fingers. In fact, he crouched down toward me, his nose sniffing the air. I stretched farther into the cage, so the part with the bars was sort of resting on my shoulder. I knew Dr. Ross would probably be mad; it'd be pretty easy for the squirrel to dart past me and be loose in the office, but I just had a feeling that it wouldn't do that. We were kindred spirits.

"Don't worry, little guy," I whispered. "I bet you're tougher than you look."

And the squirrel was beautiful. His tail was full and fluffy, like a pulled apart cotton ball. Maybe some people would think the red eyes were creepy. But those people were wrong, because they weren't creepy. They were just different. Like rubies instead of boring brown spots.

"I bet they're going to name you something stupid because of your fur. Something like Snowball or Marsh-mallow." The idea made me mad. "Not me. I'm going to call you Chuck. It's a strong, don't-mess-with-me name."

Without even thinking about it, I ran my finger down Chuck's back. He was silkier than I thought he'd be, like someone who used too much conditioner and didn't rinse it all out. He didn't move away from my finger, letting me run it down his back again and again. I didn't even realize it, but I was talking to him, too.

"Don't worry," I said. "No one thought I could do anything on my own, either. But I found a friend. Then

I found more people I liked. I made a home here, by myself. Some people still think I can't do it. They think I need to go to a special school. But I know better, just like you know better. I'm going to finish my essay, even if Sandi's idea is better and even if Kerica can't help and even if I've only been here a couple months. I'm going to finish and maybe even win, and then everyone will know that I'm fine, fine, fine. And Mom will keep getting stronger. And James won't be so scared. And Dad will come home more. And it'll all be because of me, because of what *I* did." My eyes blurred for some stupid reason and I blinked them dry again. "That's what you need to do, too. Okay? You just need to find a friend. And then you need to make a home here."

"Alice?"

I whipped my head around and there they all were—Sarah, James, Mom, and Dr. Ross. How much had they heard? I guess I panicked a little because my fingers flexed and I sort of knocked Chuck.

He made this loud whistle sound and then *bam!*

Chuck's horrible rodent teeth of pain latched onto my finger! Oh, the betrayal!

"Aaaahhh!" I jerked my finger back but Chuck didn't let go! His jaws stayed locked around my finger even as I yanked my arm backward, sending the top of the cage clattering to the floor.

"Aaaahh!" I screamed louder but all Mom, Dr. Ross, James, and Sarah did was stare as I whipped my hand—Chuck attached—in front of me.

"AAAAAHHHHH!" What could I do? I'm not sure why spinning around in a circle seemed like a good idea, but it did. It totally did. So I spun, maybe like three times, still screaming. Still with a *rodent attached to my finger.*

Suddenly the others launched toward me. Mom grabbed my arms, stopping me midtwirl. That's when Chuck's vise grip on my finger loosened and he flew across the room.

"Gotcha!" Dr. Ross said. He actually caught that stupid squirrel in the air! I heard him latch shut the cage door. "It's all right everyone! I've got him!"

"IT'S ALL RIGHT?!" I held up my hand in the air. Blood poured out of the bite marks on both sides of my finger, running down my arm and across Mom's hands. "I was bit by a squirrel. I'm *never* going to be all right!"

"Calm down, Alice." Mom twisted my hand in hers and studied the bite mark. "It looks pretty deep."

"Calm down!" I repeated.

"You're lucky he was still a little stunned," Sarah said, moving closer toward me. "He could've bit the tip of your finger right off."

"Lucky!" What was wrong with these people?

Here's the good news: No one has ever gotten rabies from a squirrel.

At least, that's what Dr. Ross said. "And Alice sort of provoked it, you know?" he added.

Whatever.

Mom, of course, called the game warden, the Department of Public Health, the pediatrician, and everyone else she could think of to confirm this. All of them said I didn't need rabies shots. I did, however, need a tetanus shot, which was literally a pain in the rump.

Here's the bad news: When you go to an urgent care center with a squirrel bite, the nurses will have a very hard time not laughing at you. In fact, they might just laugh right in your face as they clean the bite. "It's just, this is our first squirrel bite."

No kidding.

Good news: I didn't need stitches.

Bad news: My pointer finger was wrapped up like a football.

"It's okay," Mom said, patting my head. "I'll help you type your essay."

"I don't care about the stupid essay."

"Yes, you do." Mom kissed the top of my head.

Bad news: Mr. Hamlin was also in urgent care. He had fallen off the dock, twisting his ankle. Mom spotted him sitting in the waiting room with Sarah as we were leaving.

"Are you okay, Mr. Hamlin?" I rushed toward him.

He stared at me a second while Mom introduced me and herself to Susan, Sarah's mom and Mr. Hamlin's daughter-in-law. Mr. Hamlin was still staring at me like he didn't know who I was. It had only been two days since I had seen him. Then, suddenly, his eyes widened and he muttered, "Gnome Girl."

"Did you knock your head?" I asked him.

"Nah, just a little twist in the ankle. What brought you here?"

Good news: Hearing the squirrel story made him laugh, even though his ankle hurt.

"Don't worry, Gnome Girl. Lots of people get bit by squirrels."

"Did one ever bite you?"

"Course not."

I was slunk down into the cushions of the couch, Tooter curled on my lap. That was another piece of good news,

I guess. Tooter was home. Dr. Ross said he wanted to stop by the next day to check on us and talk about his observation, and Mom said he was waiving the boarding fee because of the whole bite thing.

Bad thing: Squirrel bites hurt. A lot. Maybe they'd hurt a little less if the people around me weren't such jerks about it.

When Dad came home that night, he was worse than the nurses, coughing chuckles into his napkin throughout dinner. "So, um, you spun in circles? And it—"

"Chuck," I muttered, trying to stab a lima bean with my fork using my left hand.

"Chuck," Dad corrected, "held on." He shook his head and turned to Mom. "And you didn't take a picture?"

"I know!" my mom, the traitor, said. She laughed into her napkin.

"Don't sweat it, Alice," James said, his mouth twitching. "Maybe you'll be like Spider-Man after he was bit. Maybe you'll get, like, super squirrelly powers."

I rolled my eyes, then busied myself inspecting a bite of chicken before tasting it.

"She'll crack all the toughest cases and bring justice, one nut at a time," Dad said, completely gasping for breath between laughs.

"Ha, ha." I took another bite.

"Uh-oh," Mom said mildly. "Looks like it's already setting in. She's eating like a squirrel."

"I despise all of you right now."

They laughed so hard I was sure James was going to throw up. He didn't, but Tooter did, right under the kitchen table. I might have been betrayed by my own kind, then turned on by my so-called family, but I still had Tooter.

Chapter Thirteen

The next morning, I woke up before Mom did. I don't know why my stupid heart thumped so much at that. It's not like I hadn't woken up before her for months. But she had been so *here* the past few days. I guess not having the radio playing in the kitchen when I woke up sort of felt like crawling up the sliding board. Just wrong.

I cracked open the door to her bedroom. The shades were all pulled shut. Tooter was curled up, snoring, at the base of her bed. Mom was a lump in the middle. I eased the door shut.

James leaned in the doorway of his bedroom across the hall, his arms crossed and bangs hanging over his forehead. He didn't say anything as I walked by, just sort of breathed angrily out of his nose. I heard his footsteps behind me as I made my way into the living room. I sunk into the couch next to Dad.

"Depression isn't easy," Dad said. In front of him lay about thirty loads of laundry. All of it wrinkled from being in the dryer or basket too long. He concentrated on smoothing out the curves of a T-shirt as he folded it, but even my so-so eyes could see the bumps pop right back. "For every two steps forward, there's one step back."

James grunted.

"Do you have something to share?" Dad asked. He was using this weird voice, this strained, trying-to-be-calm voice. It wouldn't take much to turn it to a yell. Both James and I knew that. James pressed his mouth shut.

"It's just—" I took a breath and started again. "She was better yesterday. She was just like *Mom* Mom." I twisted a loose piece of tape on my football finger. The bite didn't hurt but sort of throbbed a little.

Dad didn't say anything. He just kept folding the laundry.

"Is it my fault? I mean, getting bit by the squirrel, did that sort of make it worse?" I studied the loose piece of tape, twisting it tighter and tighter.

"No," Dad snapped. "It had nothing to do with you. If anything, it was a nice diversion. Your mom? She's sick. It started when we were back in Seattle and moving here just made it more obvious. Like any sicknesses, it takes time to heal." He patted a huge pile of towels down so they wouldn't tip. "All we can do is make things as easy as possible for her so she can get strong again."

"Whatever."

Both Dad and I swiveled toward James. He sat with his knees pulled up to his chest on the recliner.

"Again," Dad clipped off the word. "Do you have something to say, son?"

"Yes, *Dad*," James answered in the same tone. "How can you tell Alice it's not her fault in one breath and then say we have to help Mom in the next. Which one is it?" James slammed his feet onto the ground and popped up. I couldn't see his expression, just that his face was a blazing red STOP sign. "Maybe if you'd take a couple mornings off and 'made things easy' a couple weeks ago, Mom would already be better. Maybe she'd be the one getting Alice around town. Maybe Tooter wouldn't be off peeing on kids. Maybe I'd . . ."

Dad watched James, his hands still holding a wrinkly T-shirt. After almost a full minute, he softly asked, "Maybe you would what?"

"Maybe I wouldn't feel so . . . so . . ."

Dad slowly stood. He took a half step toward James, dropping the T-shirt. "So what?"

"So completely ANGRY!" And then James did something I've never seen before. My big brother cried like a baby. All the times I had seen him curl into himself. All the times I had seen his face shutter closed. That was nothing. This was an avalanche. A volcano. A total meltdown. My brother's fury melted into sorrow, and it poured out over my dad.

And my dad. Maybe James was right and Dad had spent the past few weeks hiding from Mom's depression, leaving us to muddle through. Or maybe he thought doing well at work was helping us. I guess it could be both. But right now, my dad was here. He was taking all that James was feeling—even now, as James pushed away Dad's embrace and kicked over the carefully stacked pile of towels. Even as Mom's door stayed shut and James went back to crying.

Finally James stopped screaming. Stopped crying even. He just sat on the floor, surrounded by clothes even more wrinkled than they had been, Dad sitting beside him and me on the couch.

"Feel better?" Dad asked.

James sort of laughed. "Yeah, I guess so."

"Good." Dad grinned. "I've been wanting to have a freak out like you just did since we moved here. I'm glad you saved me the trouble." He grabbed a T-shirt from the ground and used the hem of it to wipe James's wet face. Then Dad rammed his hands through his hair. "You're right, you know. I should've been here more. And I don't know what will help Mom. The medicine seems to be helping, but it's going to be a while till she's entirely well."

Dad flashed a smile my way. "But it's not our fault she's sick. She's always had bouts of sadness. She's just always kicked them sooner than this. She'll find her way."

Dad threw the T-shirt in his hands at James's face. "And you'll clean up this mess. Put it away when you're done."

"Where are you going?" James groaned, but he already was gathering armloads of clothes and shoving them into the laundry basket.

"I'm taking Alice to the library. She has an essay to write."

I shook my head. "I'm not doing it. It's pointless. There is no way I'm going to win."

"You're doing it."

"Why is everyone suddenly so interested in the stupid contest? Don't we have more important things to worry about?"

"Like what?" James asked, now pretending the laundry basket was a basketball net and our clothes the ball. He did a little fist bump in the air when his shot landed in the basket.

"Like Elizabeth McAllister suing us?"

Dad's smile twisted a little on his face. "Yeah," he muttered. "Definitely not out of the woods there." He balled up a pair of boxers and threw it in the basket.

"But sitting around at home working ourselves up about it isn't going to make it go away." He glanced at the clock on the wall. "We leave in five, Alice. Get your stuff."

I walked into the library and breathed in the cloud of lavender. I braced myself for Mrs. Dexter. I was sure she was going to yell at me again about pretending Tooter was a guide dog. But instead, she just said quietly, "Good morning, Alice."

Funny, I used to smell the Mill mixed in with the lavender, but now all I smelled was the flower. Strange how you get used to things.

I guess I was excited to see Kerica, because I was sort of skipping toward the hand chairs. It had only been a week since I had seen her, but it felt a lot longer. I couldn't wait to tell her about the squirrel bite. I was sure it would make her laugh. And I'll admit it: I was sort of smiling to myself. It *was* a pretty funny story. I mean, how many people can say they were bit by a squirrel? I was pretty sure I was the only one in Sinkville. I sort of snorted out loud as I thought about adding that to my Sinkville Success Stories.

Right after my profile of Mr. Hamlin spending his days whittling on the deck over the waters that sent his son to college and before the piece on how Mayor Hank brought the civil rights movement to the Williams Diner, I'd sandwich how two albinos truly came together at Dr. Ross's animal rescue.

"Something funny?" I didn't need to look to know who was behind the snide voice. Sandi was sitting at the long desk beside the hand chairs, surrounded by sheets of typewritten papers and an open laptop. Her arms were crossed as she glared at me.

"Nothing I'd like to share with you." I crossed my arms and my cane sort of flew upward.

"Need the cane now that your so-called guide dog is out of commission?"

I'm pretty sure puffs of smoke came out my nose at that; I was so furious. But being really angry shuts down my ability to think. I swear, it makes my tongue swell so that anything witty I might want to say doesn't bubble out of my mouth until the next day. Usually while I'm lying in bed trying to go to sleep and replaying the conversation. But I couldn't let her have the last word, so I said the only thing I could, lame as it was: "I don't want to talk with you."

"Suit yourself." Sandi leaned back over her papers and picked up a pencil. I had to move past her to get to the hand chairs, so I could see that she had scrawled swirls and circles all over the notes that I'm sure her mom's secretary had typed up for her. The Word document on the laptop was blank. Sandi's legs drummed up and down under the table. I smiled a little to myself. Looks like her essay wasn't going well.

I dumped my backpack in one of the hand chairs and moved toward the shelves of books looking for Kerica. I was halfway through the children's section and still hadn't spotted her when Mrs. Morris came out of her office. "Alice!" she boomed. I could hear the smile in her voice. "I am so glad to see you. How are you? How is Tooter?"

She moved closer and wrapped me in her wide arms.

"I'm fine. Tooter's fine, too. My dad dropped me off today." I looked over her shoulder. "I can't find Kerica, though. Did she come with you today?"

For a second, Mrs. Morris's smile faltered. "Yeah, she's here, but she's researching something over in the adult nonfiction section. I'm sure she'll be back in no time. Sarah Hamlin was in earlier and told us all about Tooter being in quarantine and . . ."

Mrs. Morris glanced down at my wrapped up finger. Dad had taken off the football bandaging and replaced it with some gauze and tape. It was still puffy, but I could move it easier today.

"She told you about the squirrel, too, didn't she?" I said.

Mrs. Morris hid her smile behind her hand. "It's okay," I grinned. "I know it's a little funny."

"Are you here to work on your essay?" Mrs. Morris asked.

"Yeah, I was wondering if I could use one of the computers here to write it?"

"Absolutely, although they're in high demand right now." I could see what she meant. Each of the half-dozen computer desks was full but one. Each occupant was a kid with notes and books on local history spread out around them. The only sound was a steady drumming of typing, peppered with the occasional sigh or the sudden tapping of fingers against the wooden top.

Unfortunately, the one open desk was right next to a table where Sandi was seated.

I'm not the fastest typist in the world, but I guess I'm better than most people. It's kind of ironic, I suppose. Mom used to make me type everything for school, starting when I was in third grade. I used to be so slow, having to put my face super close to the keyboard, then checking the screen to make sure the right letters showed up, then going back to the keyboard. It took forever. I hated Mom for it. But after a while, I got faster, especially once she made me do these online typing programs. Now I can type faster than I can write.

I was lost in the Williams Diner story, writing about how all the mill workers come together for milkshakes after their shifts, when I heard a snooty sigh over my shoulder. "You've been typing for, like, fifteen minutes. How in the world are you on page six already?"

Sandi was glaring at the corner of the computer screen, where I guess it said which page I was on. I couldn't make out that area well. I didn't want to answer her, but when I looked over my shoulder, I felt a pang of sympathy. Her bangs were sticking straight up from where she had pulled her hands through her hair. There was an ink splotch on her bottom lip where she must've been chewing on her pen. Her eyes were red from being rubbed.

"It's the font." I changed it back to the usual 12 from my 36. "What is it now?"

"One page," Sandi sighed.

"Well, I am working with one less finger." I grimaced in her direction, but she wasn't looking. Sandi trudged back to her seat and slumped down.

I ignored her and went back to writing. Now I was onto how the diner was the scene for a civil rights demonstration that ended with town support and the hiring of an awesome chef. Every once in a while, I'd hear a deep sigh from Sandi or the crumpling of paper.

I was almost done with this first section of my essay when Kerica returned.

"Kerica!" I jumped up in my seat, sending my note-book flying. She paused, as if she stood super still I wouldn't see her, then picked up the notebook and put it back on my desk. She was holding a huge book open and her eyes darted faster than mine.

"Are you looking for someone?" I asked.

"Mom. Have you seen her?" Kerica shifted the book so it was sort of behind her. I caught a glimpse of it, though. It looked like some sort of medical book.

"What are you reading?" I asked. Kerica went up on her tiptoes to look over my head.

"Just a book," she muttered. "I was looking for anatomy books so I could paint hands better and came across this veterinary book."

I pointed to the Post-it Notes sticking out of the sides. "Looks like you found some interesting things. Now that you've read all the dog stories, are you on to serious nonfiction?" I laughed, but Kerica's return smile was a little crooked.

"Have you seen my mom?" she repeated.

"Uh, a few minutes ago." I put my hand on her shoulder to lower her down, forcing her to look at me. "Are you all right?"

Kerica's eyes locked with mine and filled with tears. She nodded, even as her chin wobbled.

"You don't seem okay." I pulled out the chair beside me. "Want to talk?"

Kerica shook her head, sending the tears spilling down her cheeks. "Not yet." She bit her lip and then shocked me by putting her arms around me and squeezing. It was a quick-as-a-bug-bite hug and somehow stung just as much, especially since she all but sprinted to the back of the library toward her mom's office afterward.

"*Freak-a-zoid*," Sandi muttered as she balled up another page of notes and tossed it toward the trashcan.

James walked me home a few hours later, the two of us trudging along in silence.

"What's new with *Sarah?*" I drew out her name into the singsong tone I knew he hated. I was trying to break up the quiet, not really to make him mad. But James glared at me like I had cut him with glass.

"I'm sorry," I whispered, not entirely sure why I was apologizing.

James stomped a little harder than necessary and picked up the pace so he was ahead of me a few steps.

"I'm sorry!" I said louder, remembering how James had burst apart earlier that morning. It was wrong to pick on him when he was just a bunch of shoved-together pieces.

Surprising me even more than when he had glared at me, James stopped and turned, facing me full on. For the second time that day, someone told me everything was okay when their eyes were filled with tears.

"No, it's not okay," I replied. "Is it Mom?"

James sighed. "No, not really. I mean, it sort of always is, isn't it?" He shoved his hands into his pockets, but I could tell they were curled into fists. "It's pretty freaking pathetic, you know, that the only person I have to talk to is my baby sister."

I wrapped my fingers around his elbow. "I'm not going to take that personally."

James coughed out a little laugh. "It's Sarah. She's going to college in the fall."

"I know. Mr. Hamlin told me."

James sidestepped out of my grip. "Yeah, well, *I* didn't know. I've spent all summer hanging out with her. Now school's going to start in a couple weeks and I'll know absolutely no one. It was a waste of time."

I didn't say anything, just tried to keep pace with James's oversized steps as much as I could.

"I mean, I know," he continued. "I know it wasn't a waste getting to know her. I know. But I just . . . I just—"

"Feel lonely," I finished for him. "Kerica and Sandi go to the Bartel School for Girls. I'm not going to know anyone in a few weeks, either."

"Yeah, but it's easier for you." James nudged me with his shoulder. "You just put yourself out there. Everyone in this stupid town knows you."

My face flushed. "I can't help it that I stand out."

"That's not what I meant," James unclenched his fists and rammed his fingers through his too-long hair. "I mean, you. They know *you*. You just start talking to anyone. It's harder for me. I mean, in Seattle we already knew everyone. I can't figure out how to start talking to people."

I nudged him back with my shoulder. By now we were right in front of the house but walking slower. I think we both wondered what we'd see once we got inside.

"It's a trick," I told him. James tilted his head toward me. "Talking to people, it's not easy for me. I have a trick. I pretend to be Mom when she was on assignment."

James stared at the front door of our Sinkville house for a second. "She was never scared of anything then."

Chapter Fourteen

The phone was ringing as we walked in the door. James rushed to answer it before the answering machine picked up. "Uh, I need to find her."

I trailed James down the hallway as he cracked open Mom's bedroom door. We both jerked our heads in surprise. The blinds were open and the windows cracked. Sunlight poured into the room I had always sort of thought of as a cave. "I'm sorry, Dr. Ross," James said. "I'm not sure where my mom is. . . . Yes. . . . I'll make sure she calls. Okay, bye."

James caught my eye. "He said he called a couple times today."

"Where's Tooter?" I clapped my hands against my knees and listened for the sound of his collar clinking.

Nothing.

Suddenly we heard a whistle and laughter from the backyard. We almost tripped over each other as we rushed to check it out. And then, as if we had run straight into fly paper, we stopped. Mom was laughing. I pushed pass James to better see.

We found Mom playing fetch with Tooter, only he wasn't doing much fetching.

"Silly pup," Mom said. I stepped out onto the back porch as she moved to gather up the balls she had already thrown. "Hey guys!" Mom called to us. "Want to help teach this old dog new tricks? He forgets how to fetch!"

James just stared at Mom, so I went to the other side of the yard. "Monkey in the middle?" I asked.

"Sure!" Soon we were putting Tooter in a frenzy, throwing the tennis ball back and forth. I only missed a couple times, but even then Tooter didn't make a move to steal the ball. It was funny; he used to grab onto tennis balls and rip them to shreds.

"He likes the anticipation more than the actual doing," Mom laughed as the ball rolled under Tooter and he still didn't pick it up. "Getting old, I guess."

Tooter twirled a couple times and settled on the grass beside the ball. I ran beside Mom, wrapping an arm around her waist as she bent to kiss the top of my head.

"Speaking of oldie moldy," Mom glanced over at James, who was still watching from the porch. "Wanna play?" She threw the ball his way and his arm shot out to grab it. He tossed it back.

"Nah," he said. "I've got to get dinner ready."

James's words slapped Mom, or at least that's how it looked to me. Her mouth popped open and closed a couple times. "That's my line, isn't it?" she half-heartedly whispered.

"He's been making dinner most nights," I reminded her.

"Hmm." She smoothed her hands across her shorts like she was pushing away her thoughts.

"Hey, Mom, can Kerica come over this weekend? Maybe Saturday?"

Mom paused. I just knew she was going to say she was too tired. But instead, she said, "Sure. I don't see why not. Let's go help James with dinner."

The table was set by the time Dad's car pulled into the garage. Mom even had James laughing as she told a story about trying to eat anything other than fermented fish in Sweden. "Swedish fish? They are nothing like the candy."

Dad walked in and glanced at the set table. "Taco Tuesday?" he asked. "Sure you can handle this, Squirrel Bait? Or are we in for another flying taco?"

"Har har." I sat down and held up my fingers in a Girl Scout salute. "I promise not to throw my plate across the room, even if the guacamole does slip out of the shell."

Even though everyone was smiling during dinner, there was still something heavy in the air. Every second that passed without someone saying something or cracking some sort of joke, the air gained weight. Finally the phone rang, breaking the silence apart as we each jumped to answer it.

Mom laughed and motioned for everyone to sit. "Ignore it. Let's just enjoy our dinner together."

James kept standing, even as the rest of us sat. Mom tugged on his fingertips. "It's okay, baby," she said, moving her hands to the sides of his face. "We're all okay."

James tilted his cheek into her hand and smiled. I let go of the breath I didn't even know I was holding.

But we weren't all okay.

The message was from Elizabeth McAllister's lawyer, Mr. Humphrey.

The next night, Dad sent James and me to our rooms while he met in the living room with Mr. Hamlin's son, Anthony Hamlin, Attorney at Law.

Mr. Humphrey, the McAllister's lawyer, had asked for Dr. Ross's medical records on Tooter. Sarah immediately told her dad and asked him to help. Anthony Hamlin looked like his whittler dad: tall and thin, solemn brown eyes, and slow smile. But really he was as different as he could be. First off was his attire. Old Mr. Hamlin wore flannel button-down shirts that were probably once deep reds and blues but were now more faded than Mom's vase of dried hydrangeas. Anthony Hamlin wore a crisp slate-gray suit and a starched white shirt. His hair was slicked back in artful swirls while his father's fluffy brown hair curled up over the edges of a faded baseball cap.

Old Mr. Hamlin seemed to me like one of his pieces of wood, steady and still. The only thing that really moved on him was his hands, and those movements were so swift and minute that if you weren't paying close attention, you'd miss them. Younger Mr. Hamlin, however, was a running brook of energy. He bounced on his heels as he met us. I heard a *click-click-click* sound from the living room as he met with Mom and Dad. It was either his heel drumming against the tiled floor or a pen cap being pressed again and again.

"How is this even possible?" Dad asked. "I mean, it's just a little dog pee. How is there a lawsuit in there?"

Anthony Hamlin laughed. "Anything can be a lawsuit. Someone actually sued NASA because the Mars Rover didn't inspect a rock closely enough for him." He paused, waiting for Mom and Dad to join in his chuckle. They didn't. Anthony Hamlin cleared his throat. "Actually, the McAllisters filed a number of suits."

Dad groaned and Mom sighed. "On what grounds?" she asked.

I heard the rustle of papers and Anthony Hamlin cleared his throat again. "They want Tooter to be classified as a dangerous dog, they're seeking enforcement of the dog barking law against you, petitioning for a criminal complaint for assault and battery, and filing a civil complaint for assault, battery, and intentional infliction of emotional distress."

"What does that even mean?" Mom exploded. "My God! The dog peed on her leg. That's assault and battery?"

"It's overwhelming, I know. The truth is, they're throwing everything against the wall here to see what sticks."

"What's going to stick?" Dad said. His voice was muffled. I could picture him sitting with his hands cupped over his mouth so only his eyes peered above his hands.

"Okay, let's break it down." *Click-click-click* from Anthony Hamlin. "To be deemed a dangerous dog, Tooter would have to attack, inflict grievous bodily injury, or kill a person. They're going to stick with the attack part of that, since clearly Sandi wasn't actually harmed or killed by the pee. Although they are saying there was a scratch."

I bunched my hands into fists. I saw Sandi yesterday. The scratch wasn't even visible! Well, not to me, anyway.

"We're not going to worry about that one." *Click-click-click*. "I represented a client a few years ago whose giant dog broke into a stranger's home, attacked his puppy, inflicted bite marks all over the stranger's hands, and invoked thousands of dollars in medical and veterinary bills. That dog didn't qualify as a dangerous dog, so no way Tooter will."

"That's good to know," Mom said in a voice that made it sound like she was saying the opposite.

Click-click-click. "Moving on, the assault and battery charges. Assault is an act that puts someone in apprehension of imminent physical harm. In other words, it makes someone feel they are going to be hurt, regardless of if that injury happens. They're going to contend that Tooter was acting vicious and his barking made Sandi perceive she was in danger. Battery is physical touching. It doesn't have to be a large injury."

"Is this where we're in trouble?" Dad asked.

"It's a bit more of a pickle on paper, that's for sure. Then there is the Dog Barking Law. It's usually landed on people who let their dogs bark in the middle of the night, but, like I said, they're going for it all here." *Click-click-click*. "I can tell you, no cop is going to pick up these charges and run with them. They'll come here, meet Tooter, and wash their hands of it. Criminal isn't going to stick."

"So civil?" Mom prompted.

"Civil. I'm sure you know this already, but suing in state court means they're going for monetary compensation. They're suing for assault and battery in civil court. The burden of proof is looser here. And they're pushing for Intentional Infliction of Emotional Distress. They've got to contend that this experience made something in Sandi change. Like she's scared to lie in the grass now or is terrified to be around dogs."

"She's exactly the same horrible, hateful person she's always been!" I shouted from the hall.

Anthony Hamlin snickered.

"What are our chances?" asked Mom, totally ignoring me.

"With me as your lawyer, excellent. This is going to fail in civil court. They're required to prove damages. What are they going to prove? That they had to wash the girl's leg? Come on. They're going to push on emotional damages, but it's still a slippery case. My gut is that Elizabeth McAllister is just being a nuisance, trying to force you to shell out cash in legal fees that aren't going to go anywhere."

Mom growled. For real. It sounded a lot like Tooter. *Click-click-click.*

"Seems like as good a time as any to ask about your legal fees," Dad said.

"Three hundred and twenty-five dollars per hour." *Click-click-click* as Dad coughed and Mom sucked in her breath. *Click-click-click.* "But I'm not charging you."

Silence. I crept down the hallway. Mom and Dad were staring at Anthony Hamlin.

"You're not going to represent us?" I again had no control of my voice. This seems to be a problem lately.

Anthony Hamlin chuckled again. "No, I'm going to represent you. I'm just going to do it pro bono. Nothing owed to me. If we lose—which we won't— you'll, of course, have to pay the damages. But I'm not charging you."

"Why not?" Dad gasped. Mom nudged him with her elbow in a don't-question-it kind of way.

"Humility and lawyering don't go hand in hand, so I'm going to say it like it is. I'm the best there is. I whooped Humphrey in court more times than I can count. I can't wait to do it again. When I file these responding papers and McAllister and Humphrey see my name at the top, they'll probably drop the charges right then and there. But crushing them again is only one small reason I'm not charging. The real reason is my dad." Anthony Hamlin shifted in his seat, tilting his head in my direction. "This girl over there and her dog melted that old wooden heart of his. He agreed to do something for me if I did this for you."

I stood there stiff as a board as Mom and Dad breathed out like they were blowing worries from a dandelion. And I knew I couldn't do it. I couldn't let Anthony Hamlin represent us.

"No." It came out as a squeak. No one heard me. I tried louder. This time it was a yell. All three of them turned toward me. I heard James's door pop open in the hall. "No. I'm sorry Mr. Hamlin, but we cannot accept. You don't owe your dad a favor anymore."

"What are you talking about, Alice?" Dad sounded stunned.

"I know the favor Mr. Hamlin—the older Mr. Hamlin—had to make. He agreed to let you sell the farmland. He's going to let you put him in an old folks' home. I can't let you do that. He needs that land for Sarah. He needs the woods and the whittling and the sunset and no creamed carrots! We don't accept."

To my surprise, Anthony Hamlin's grin only spread. He came down and knelt in front of me. "He told me you'd say that." He shook his head. "My old man finally met someone as stubborn as he is. Dad's not selling the land. He's putting it in a trust for Sarah, whom I hope *will* agree to sell it instead of follow through on her farm scheme."

"It's not a scheme." James stepped out of the hall. "It's going to be an organic farm."

Anthony Hamlin's chipper face turned stony for a second and he rose to his feet. "We'll see," he said, and then knelt beside me again. "Dad *wants* to go into the Bartel Retirement Village. There he can make friends and have plenty of folks checking in on him."

"I check on him." I shifted a little, realizing that came out a little rude. "I'm his friend."

"I know you are." Anthony Hamlin patted my head. I hate when grown-ups do that.

"No, thank you. I do not accept your terms." I was pretty sure Dad had stopped breathing. Mom was fanning him with her hands. But I just kept thinking of that morning when I had stopped by Mr. Hamlin's. I had knocked on the door and he had stumbled out with a cane. We did a cane high-five and he opened the door wider to let me in, but I could tell he had just been sleeping—he was still in his pajamas. So I had left. But he was fine. Just fine.

Again Anthony Hamlin just smiled. "It's not up to you."

He shook Mom and Dad's hands and promised we had nothing to worry about.

Chapter Fifteen

Saturday morning, I tried to clean up the house a little before Kerica came over. The biggest thing to tackle was Mom's big box of newspaper clippings and note-books, still in our hallway. I found Mom's journal from when I was a baby tucked in the back of the box.

I flipped through it, reading snippets about colic and sleepless nights, cuddling with James, and my first laugh. Somehow I ended up on the page—the one from when a doctor told them I was blind and that there wasn't anything they could do about it. Here's what she wrote:

A thunderstorm of disconnected thoughts raged through my head—Seeing Eye dogs and special schools, the clutter we'd seriously need to address in the house. I thought of the things this precious child would miss. The beauty of a sunrise, going to the movies, finding a familiar face in a crowd, losing herself in the pages of a book. I cursed myself for missing this for four months. How does a mother not realize her baby is blind?

"Don't worry, Dana," Ted said as we pulled out of the office parking lot. *"We'll deal with it."* His eyes met mine in the rearview mirror. *"We'll teach her all about the three visually impaired mice."*

Despite myself, I laughed.

A few days later, Mom was on the phone with Dr. Ross when I got home from the library. "Yes. Next week is pretty clear, except we have an appointment on Thursday. Tomorrow? Oh. Okay. Fine. See you in the afternoon."

"Everything okay?" Tooter finished quarantine. Why was Dr. Ross calling?

"Yeah, Dr. Ross just wants to give Tooter a checkup. We've been a little lax." Mom scribbled the appointment time on the calendar stuck to the fridge. "Guess he's due for vaccines and everything."

"He's pretty insistent about it," James said. He grabbed a bag of corn chips from the pantry and tore into them, even though Mom was chopping vegetables for the dinner we'd have soon.

Mom chopped a little faster. "During the whole inspection period, where Dr. Ross stopped by every day, he thought he saw a few things with Tooter."

"What things?" I asked. Hearing his name, Tooter scooted on his butt across the kitchen tiles and then sat on my feet with a fart.

Mom sighed and James threw Tooter a chip like a reward. It hit Tooter in the head. He sniffed then chomped down on it. "Apparently typical Tooter stuff," she gestured toward the dog with her chopping knife, "is odd dog stuff. So he wants him to have a checkup."

I watched Tooter sniff around for crumbs and shrugged. He was a strange dog. But weren't we all a little strange?

"What's going on Thursday?" I asked, remembering Mom saying we had an appointment. The *we* part was kind of strange. I mean, I know she had a lot of appointments because of her depression, even though she finally seemed to be Seattle Mom all the time now. But *we* didn't have appointments.

Both James and Mom turned to statues for a second, Mom with her knife frozen over carrots, James with his lips around a corn chip. "Just an appointment," Mom said, resuming chopping.

"Hey, I just remembered," James burst out before I could ask Mom why she was being so vague. "Chuck's in love. Unfortunately, it's with my girlfriend."

"Girlfriend?" Mom choked out.

James ignored her. "Check it out." He handed me his phone. I slipped my magnifier out of my pocket to enlarge the picture of Chuck sitting on Sarah's shoulder. "Turns out," James said, "Chuck's pretty sweet. If you don't provoke him."

Jerk. I probably would've pummeled him for that if the house phone hadn't rung again.

Mom answered it, still laughing about Chuck's romance. "Hi there! . . . Sure. Hang on just a sec." She held out the phone toward me. "It's for you."

"Hey, Kerica!" I said into the phone, figuring it was her since she's the only one who calls me.

"Um, it's Eliza."

I sucked in my breath. "Oh. Hi," I said.

Eliza's words tumbled out of the phone. I could tell she was bouncing in place. "Look, I feel really badly about what I said last time we talked. I didn't think about how it would sound to you. I miss you, Alice, I do. I just meant—"

"Slow down, Eliza. It's okay." I turned, feeling James's and Mom's eyes on me. I waited to hear Mom get back to chopping and James talking with her about Sarah. "I just was feeling lonely and it felt like you were moving on—"

"But you're still my friend!" Eliza said.

"I know," I said, remembering what I had told Kerica about friends being able to fight and still make up. "You're my friend, too. So, how was that party?"

After dinner, Dad and I went to visit Mr. Hamlin at Bartel Village. Dad said he wanted to thank him for raising such a good lawyer. It turns out that the morning I had visited Mr. Hamlin—when he was still in his pajamas—he hadn't been sleeping. He had been packing. Already he had a room at the old folks' home.

His son moved just as fast. "Anthony already got the criminal charges dismissed!" Dad reached behind him to fist bump me in the backseat but I wasn't paying attention. He ended up tugging my leg instead. "Come on, kid! That's got to be deserving of a cheer. Just the civil suit left and we're in the clear."

"Huzzah." Of course I was beyond relieved that we only had the civil charges to deal with, but it wasn't enough to make me feel better about Mr. Hamlin being in the old folks' home. Thinking about it made my heart sink, like it was being filled with lake water.

Would he be able to whittle there? How would he get his wood? I sighed, wishing I would've grabbed some from the backyard before we left. We should've brought *something* to cheer him up.

Almost like he read my thoughts—or maybe because he's just not capable of driving by without stopping—Dad pulled into the Williams Diner. "Let's get a milkshake for Mr. Hamlin," he suggested.

"And a couple for us."

"Of course."

Mayor Hank sat at the counter next to a kid I had seen at the library next to a stack of local history books. The boy was furiously typing into a laptop and firing questions at the mayor.

"Ah, the competition," Dad said as we slid into a booth.

I shrugged. "Lots of kids are entering the contest."

"Did you finish typing yours yet?" Dad asked.

I shook my head.

"I'm sure you'll do great," Dad said without looking up from the milkshake menu. "You've got your mother's talent."

I didn't say anything, trying to listen to what the kid was asking Mayor Hank. It sounded like he wanted to know a lot about the Bartel family. Kind of the obvious way to go, I told myself, even as I mentally kicked myself for not doing the same. I mean, just about everything in the whole darn town was named for the paper mill owners, and I had nothing—*nothing*—about the family in my research.

Again I thought of Sandi and her interviews with representatives and even a senator.

What was I thinking, doing a Sinkville Success Stories essay without mentioning one famous or prominent person? I guess I had Mayor Hank, but only from when he was a newbie in town.

"I don't think I'm going to finish the essay," I said, not looking up from my menu.

Dad slapped the laminated paper to the tabletop. He didn't say anything, just arched a fuzzy eyebrow at me.

I glanced around to make sure Gretel wasn't nearby, even though I could hear her in the kitchen. "Look," I whispered, "Sandi interviewed famous people. The kid over there is researching the Bartels. All I've got are interviews. One with an old man in an old folks' home. Another with a milkshake maker. And one with a mayor talking about when he was a teenager. I've got a story about a deranged albino squirrel and other rejects at the sanctuary. Basically, nothing worth writing about." I sat back in the booth and squeezed my eyes shut. When I am upset, my eyes flutter like crazy and I knew Dad was tuned into that.

He moved from his side of the booth and slipped into my side. He kissed the tip of my nose. "Every time your mom wrote an article, she was sure it was going to get her fired. She never mentioned the usual touristy spots or ate in the fancy restaurants." Dad sat back and smiled; I knew he was thinking of Mom with her camera around her neck and her notebook in her hands. "She found the real people, the real stories. And you know what? That's what made her so good."

He squeezed my hand and went back to his side of the booth as Gretel sauntered up to our table. "You're getting the fruit smoothie with spinach. No arguing," she told Dad, pointing at him with her pen. Her velvety voice still made me break out in chills, thinking of Grandma. "Can't have my best customer going and getting diabetes on me." She turned to me. "You, my darling girl. You can have anything you'd like."

Before I could order, she turned toward Mayor Hank. "But make it quick. As soon as that kid's done talking to Harold, we're outta here. Got a date." She winked at me.

I popped up and squeezed Gretel into a quick hug. "Yes!" I cheered.

Gretel smiled and popped her pen cap, ready to write down my order.

"What's Mr. Hamlin's favorite shake?"

"Vanilla with a dash of caramel sauce," she answered immediately.

"I'll take one of those for me and one to go for him."

She smiled at me. "I'll make it with extra love. Be sure to tell him that."

After Gretel disappeared back in the kitchen, Dad smiled at me for so long that I was the one arching a fuzzy eyebrow in his direction. "What?"

"Just love you, kiddo," he said. "That's all."

I took a deep breath as we walked up to the glass doors of Bartel Village.

It didn't look like an old folks' home. Really, it looked like a beautiful white house. A wide ramp led to a huge wraparound porch, with loads of wooden rocking chairs and pots of flowers. We passed a few people in wheelchairs, staring out across the parking lot like they were waiting for a visitor.

Inside, Dad signed a guest register as I watched fish swimming in a big tank. A lady leaned on the arms of a metal walker beside me, a curled-up finger tracing the route a bright yellow fish was taking through the water. "Blub, blub," she muttered.

I chewed my lip and turned away. "Mr. Hamlin's on the second floor," Dad said, grabbing my hand. I'm a little old for hand holding, but I didn't let go.

A photograph of Mr. Hamlin was taped to the door of his room. It was of him sitting on the dock, whittling knife and wood in his hands. Dad knocked on the door and eased it open. "Hmm," he said when no one was inside.

A nurse walking by smiled at us and said, "You looking for Mike Hamlin? He's doing arts hour in the cafeteria."

She gave Dad directions while I squeezed my eyes shut, trying to picture old folks' art hour. What would they be doing? Knitting doilies? Poor Mr. Hamlin was probably sitting in a dark corner, remembering his lake, missing his whittling. And all I had for him was a stupid milkshake. "Let's just go home," I nudged Dad.

He ignored me, grabbing my arm and leading us to the cafeteria. I opened my eyes and sucked in my breath. The cafeteria was huge, with dozens of little round tables. The room was drenched with light from huge floor-to-ceiling windows. And yes, the table in front of us was filled with ladies knitting. But other people were painting or drawing with tabletop easels or sculpting clay on small trays. And everywhere was laughter and chattering.

"Is that him?" Dad pointed to a table by the window. I sort of shrugged. The man was too far to see for sure and Dad, who had never met Mr. Hamlin, was just going by the photograph he had seen on the door. Dad moved forward, but the closer we got the less I thought it could be Mr. Hamlin. This man was sketching.

Beside him, a man with a wild fluff of gray hair was telling bad jokes about pirates' favorite letters ("*R*," answered the Maybe Mr. Hamlin. "Nope, a pirate's first love is always the *C*! Ha!") and the Maybe Mr. Hamlin was belly laughing in a way I had never heard before.

But when I got close enough, I knew it was Actual Mr. Hamlin. He was wearing the same thin flannel shirt as last time I saw him and he smelled the same, like wood shavings and pine. His back was to me, but I recognized his hand, now gripping a charcoal pencil instead of a knife. He was shading in a drawing so realistic of the dock that I forgot he didn't know I was there and moved closer to see all of it. My face was just a few inches from the paper, looking at the little girl and the dog sitting at the edge of the dock, when I felt Mr. Hamlin's hand cup the back of my head. "Gnome Girl," he said, and I could tell he was smiling.

I turned and, surprising us both, I hugged him. "I brought you a milkshake," I said into his bony shoulder.

"Made with extra love, I hope."

I nodded and leaned back so I could see his face. Mr. Hamlin was smiling, too big and easy to be fake. "Meet my friends," he said. "This here is Pat Winchester. We went to high school together. You believe that?"

Mr. Winchester, the pirate joke teller, grinned at me, popping his fake teeth out and back again. Guess that's the thing for old men to do when they meet girls.

"Haven't seen Pat in, what? Twenty years?"

"Not since before Margi passed," the comedian said.

Mr. Hamlin introduced us to a half-dozen other "old buddies," but I was too busy watching the whittler's face to be polite. When was he going to drop this happy act? Sure this place was sunny and bright. But it wasn't our lake. It wasn't the dock.

I was still watching Mr. Hamlin a half-hour later when Dad excused himself to go to the restroom. Art hour had ended and the cafeteria was mostly empty.

"Relax, Gnome Girl." Mr. Hamlin patted the top of my head. "I like it here."

"You said you never wanted to go to an old folks' home."

He nodded. "I didn't. But then I busted my ankle." He ran a finger along the deep, still healing cut in his left palm. "Sliced up my hand. Can't whittle. Sarah's about to go to college. Tony's too busy lawyerin'. I'd be a pathetic old man on the dock if I weren't here."

I shook my head. "I'd visit you. Me and Tooter."

"Ain't Tooter on house arrest? And you'd be in Columbia in a few weeks at that fancy school."

I felt all the blood in my face rush to my feet. Somehow between Tooter and the essay, I had forgotten all about the school for the blind, even though that's all I had talked about to Mr. Hamlin a few weeks ago. "I told you: I'm not going there!"

Mr. Hamlin shrugged. "Okay." He sighed and lay his arms out across his chair. "You know, I used to get up. Eat alone. Whittle alone, unless you or Sarah swung by. Eat alone again. Rock alone. Eat alone again. Sleep alone. And I was sure as sunshine it was what I wanted."

I didn't answer him, just shook my head.

"Then I come here. Only been two days and I already got a routine. Eat breakfast with my buddies. Do stuff. You know, bingo, cards, or drawing. Work on getting my ankle fixed up. Have lunch with my friends. Read or nap or chitchat. It's not bad." He rolled over to the little desk in the corner and grabbed a piece of paper. "Check this out," he said, handing me a Bartel Village flyer including a packed schedule of activities. "All these things I can do." He flipped it over and pointed to a long list of volunteer positions. "All these people who come in to help us old farts have fun."

"You miss the lake. You miss your house. I know you do." I had been so worried he was miserable here, wasting away alone. Here Mr. Hamlin was telling me he was happy. Showing me that he was happy. And now

I was trying to convince him he was sad. I hated the boiling mush feeling in my chest as I spit out my words but I couldn't stop.

Mr. Hamlin nodded. "That I do. But that doesn't mean I can't like it here." He gave me a crooked smile. "You know, I actually thought I wasn't old enough to live here. Now I sort of wish I had been here sooner. You know, before I developed bad habits. Like stubbornness."

I looked at my feet. "I'm not blind enough for that stupid school."

"Maybe." Mr. Hamlin nodded. "Or maybe not. Won't know 'til you check it out, though."

Dad came back. He pushed Mr. Hamlin's wheelchair back to his room. I tried not to look at Mr. Hamlin when he was in the chair. It was too hard to picture him going over the roots and rocks on the trail to the dock in a wheelchair. I knew he wouldn't be able to do it.

I stared at the flyer he handed me and its long list of activities and volunteers. "Can I keep this?"

"Sure, Gnome Girl. Got something else for you, too, 'less you're sick of these pieces of junk." Mr. Hamlin grabbed something from his dresser and held it out for me.

It was a perfectly whittled Tooter. The little statue dog's mouth was hanging open and its tail bent mid-wag. I squeezed it in my hand and kissed him on the cheek. "You're happy."

It was a statement, not a question, but he nodded. "I'm happy. Be even happier if you visit soon."

"I'll check on you often," I promised.

Chapter Sixteen

When you were a reporter, how did you know what to write about?" I asked Mom. We were curled on the couch, both of us tired and in our pajamas but not ready to go to bed.

She smiled and pulled my head against her shoulder. "I thought about your dad. What would be the first thing I'd tell him about the trip I was on? That was where I would start my story."

"I feel like my story's not important."

"You're writing about people. And every story about a person is important. To someone, that story is everything."

"Can I show you something?" I pulled out the Bartel Village flyer from my pocket. I had circled an open volunteer position. "They're looking for someone to interview residents. To find out their stories and write them down. Maybe even to photograph them."

Mom took the flyer from me. Her eyes fluttered to me then the flyer and back. "I think that'd be a pretty big undertaking for a young girl."

"But maybe not for a journalist mom." I kissed her cheek and went to bed, not bothering to scour the newspaper for job openings on the way.

The next morning, Mom dropped me off at the library on her way to the vet's with Tooter. Sinkville Success Stories contest entries had to be emailed to Mayor Hank's office by midnight and I had only gotten through writing Mr. Hamlin's part. And not even really that. I wanted to add about him finding happiness in Bartel Village. I still had to write about Williams Diner and the Sycamore, plus I wanted to add a section on Dr. Ross's work with abandoned animals. "Good luck," Mom said as I got out of the car. Tooter farted.

I stationed myself at the computer desk, earbuds in and iPod on, trying to block out everyone and everything. Unfortunately, Sandi was at the computer next to mine. "My laptop keyboard is too small," she whined as I sat down, as if I cared.

Still, I couldn't block out that for every word I typed, she sighed. Coughed. Twitched. Broke pencils. Ripped up paper.

Mrs. Morris, who had told me Kerica stayed home to work on a project, walked by a couple times.

I figured that meant she was working on the painting for the Williams Diner. Mrs. Morris kept patting Sandi's shoulder and whispering things like, "You can do it!" and "Keep your chin up." Sandi kept right on biting her nails, drumming her fingers onto the tabletop, and cracking her knuckles. Everything but writing her essay.

After two hours of this, I couldn't help myself. I asked her if she was okay.

"I'm fine," she snapped. And then burst into tears.

Sandi couldn't type. Not really a sob-worthy thing, if you ask me. But Sandi was a blubbering mess, her tears pouring over her hands as she rocked back and forth in her computer seat.

"So what?" I said. "Lots of people can't type. Just write it out and maybe someone will type it up for you."

"Ahbanniteiteiter."

"What?" I pulled Sandi's hands from her face.

Much softer, head still down, she repeated. "I can't write, either."

"You're being hard on yourself," I said. "I know how much research you've done. You've just got to write it."

Sandi stopped hiccupping. She lifted her face and pierced me with red-rimmed eyes. "I. Can't. Write."

My vision problem? That's because my eyes don't have enough pigment to send whole picture messages down my optic nerves. The nystagmus—the twitchy movement of my eyes—is my brain's way of trying to get more information, trying to focus. I can't ever fully focus, but my brain never stops trying.

Sandi's brain never stops trying to turn letters into words, even though somewhere between when her eyes see the letters and the time that message gets to her brain, the message gets mixed up. She has something called dyslexia. And just like I'm toward the worst-you-can-get part of the albinism spectrum, she's got a bad case of dyslexia. Her essay was in her head, but it scattered by the time it got to paper.

"Is it something you were born with?" I asked.

Sandi shrugged. "I guess so. Mom just thought I was stupid and lazy. Kept telling me to try harder when I was learning to read, then sent me to a bunch of tutors. Mrs. Morris helps a lot. She says I'm harder working than anyone she's ever taught." Sandi lifted her chin like she expected me to disagree. "She even told my mom that."

"Can I ask you something?"

"If it's about your stupid dog, forget it. I'm sorry, but my mom's really mad about it and she doesn't get over stuff easily."

I bit my lip hard enough to sting and shook my head. "I think you and your mom are being jerks about Tooter, but that's not what I was going to ask."

Sandi rolled her eyes and tilted her chin in a go-ahead sort of way.

"Why are you doing the essay? I mean, it's voluntary, right? Why would you volunteer to make yourself miserable?"

"Same reason as anyone." Sandi rubbed at her eyes with her sleeve cuff. "The prize money. Isn't that why you're doing it? I mean, that'd cover some legal fees."

I bit my lip again and shook my head. "I'm doing it because . . ." I started to say something untrue and, okay, a little snobby. Like, *because I love Sinkville and want to celebrate its successes.* But she was being honest, so I could, too. "So I could prove to everyone that I could do it. Mostly prove it to my mom."

Sandi's smile spread slowly until it covered her whole face. "That's pretty much why I do everything."

"You've got tons of money," I pointed out. Sandi nodded. "Why do you want the prize money?"

Sandi's face stiffened and I knew she was about to say something mean. But she shook her head and then told the truth. "Mom bought me an American Girl doll when I failed kindergarten. I mean, seriously. Who fails kindergarten? Jeremy Rogers ate an entire bottle of glue and he passed kindergarten. When I had to quit cheerleading because I couldn't remember the chants, she bought me a new wardrobe. When Bartel School for Girls suggested I find a place 'more appropriate to my needs,' Mom bought them a new library and hired Mrs. Morris to be my tutor. If there is a problem, she throws money at it."

I nodded, waiting for her to continue.

"I'm going to give the money to Mom. I'm going to tell her she's the problem."

We stared at each other for a full minute.

"I'm going to buy my mom a ton of new notebooks." Mom had called Bartel Village and was scheduled to interview a lady on Tuesday. I wanted to buy her a bunch of notebooks, hoping she wouldn't stop with just one person's story. I didn't want to explain it, so I turned back to my computer. Already typing, I said, "I'm almost done with my essay. Then I'm going to type yours."

"The contest is closed to partners." Sandi turned back to her computer, too, her shoulders slumping as she shut it down.

I grabbed her wrist and pulled her back into her seat as she stood to zip shut her backpack. "I'm not going to be your partner. I'm going to type everything you say, as you say it."

"Why would you do that?"

I shrugged. "Because I want to."

It took about four hours. Sandi even ordered lunch, probably the first time a pizza was ever delivered to the library. I've got to hand it to her, she handled Mrs. Dexter like an expert. "What is this?" Mrs. Dexter had asked as the pizza delivery guy walked in with a large pepperoni pie.

"This is called pizza, Mrs. Dexter." Sandi handed the guy cash.

"This is a library!"

"And this is a pizza!" Sandi opened the box, releasing a heavenly aroma of melted cheese and sauce. "Have a slice." She put a piece right into Mrs. Dexter's outraged hands.

I've got to admit, Sandi's essay was good. She pinpointed all the awesome things Sinkville leaders had done—the way they kept taxes low but the schools great, the way representatives made sure park land was preserved and crime prevented. She pointed out the high voting rates and the profitable business. I shifted a little in my seat, realizing her essay was pretty much the exact opposite of mine. The coolest part? She never looked at her notes once. Maybe that's because they were in pieces all over the desk, but more likely, I think, because she really got into the topic. I almost interrupted her to say that if she ever ran for office, I'd vote for her. But I kept typing, just as she said it, and then read it back to her when we were done.

Both of us sighed as we hit "send" on our essays. We made the deadline.

"What now?" I asked, rubbing my fingers. I must've typed three thousand words that afternoon. By "what now," I meant what was next for us? Would we go back to ignoring each other? To her mom suing my parents? Were we—gasp!—becoming friends?

Sandi snagged a pepperoni from the last remaining slice of pizza in the box. She nibbled on it for a second then said, "The essays are vetted through a group of townspeople. The finalists' essays are put up on the website and printed in the *Sinkville Gazette*. People vote on them and the finalists find out who wins at a reception next month."

"That's not what I meant—" But Kerica interrupted me before I could finish.

"Alice?" she asked in a shaky voice.

For some reason, I felt like I was being a traitor to Kerica, sitting here eating pizza with Sandi. I even stood up. "Hey, Kerica!" I said way too brightly. "Your mom said you were working on a project at home."

Kerica shook her head, rattling her braids. "Not really. I just. I need to talk with you."

Kerica had taken the bus in from Columbia by herself after her mom told her I was at the library. "I've been avoiding you, but that's not right. I need to tell you something. I've been doing a lot of reading about dogs. I mean nonfiction reading." I nodded, knowing she had read every single fiction book about dogs in the library by the end of June. "Mom loves your dog and I thought if I did a lot of research, maybe I could finally convince her to get a dog, too."

"Okay," I had said slowly.

"I came across something in a veterinary book. Something about tumors. I think . . ." She swallowed and started again. "I think Tooter has a brain tumor."

It fit, she said. During the past few weeks, she had noticed the way Tooter had changed. The way he suddenly couldn't jump into the hand chairs. The way he paced in circles sometimes. The strange reaction to Sandi. Even how he peed on her and everything else. The way his back legs would sometimes go limp and I'd carry him. It wasn't just an odd dog being weird.

The more she talked, the more I hated her. Who did she think she was, diagnosing my dog with a tumor? She's a kid, like me, not a vet! She doesn't know Tooter, how he's always been quirky. He's my dog! I'd know if he was sick, not some stranger.

But being mad was harder than it should've been, as my mind snapped back to Dr. Ross leaving messages. To Tooter growling at James a few days ago. To thinking about how maybe he wasn't scooting across the floor to be lazy. Maybe it was because his legs weren't working right. Maybe Kerica was right. Maybe she saw what we couldn't. What we wouldn't.

I stood up, right in the middle of Kerica saying she was so, so sorry. "Will you walk me home?"

She stopped midsentence and nodded. I grabbed my notebook, shoved it in my backpack, and moved toward the doors. Kerica shadowed me, not standing close or touching. It was like an invisible wall suddenly popped between us.

Sandi stepped into my path. I tried to step around her, trying to wall her away, too.

Sandi wrapped her hand around my wrist, even as Kerica rushed to my side. "We're dropping the suit."

"Do you really think this is the time?" Kerica's voice, still shaky, morphed into the snobby tone she always took with Sandi.

But Sandi didn't even glance her way. "I'm going to tell my mom what you did for me today. I'm going to get her to drop the suit. I'm not going to stop until she does."

And then the strangest thing ever happened. Sandi gave me a hug. And the wall between me and Kerica dissolved. Kerica slipped her hand into mine and she and Sandi walked me home.

Mom sat on the couch holding Tooter. I could smell bacon as I opened the door and could tell from Tooter's happy slurping sounds that she was feeding it to him.

I didn't have to get close to see that Mom was crying. My friends stopped at the doorway when they saw her and both of them quietly left. I don't even know if they said good-bye.

"It's a brain tumor," I said. Mom didn't seem surprised that I knew. I thought about how she had dodged Dr. Ross for so long and suspected that it wasn't all that surprising to her, either.

I sat down beside them on the ground, burying my hands into Tooter's fur. "Is he going to die?"

Mom pet the back of my head in a copy of how I was petting Tooter. "He's thirteen years old, Sunshine," she told me. "He's been dying for a while."

"What can we do?"

"Make the most of the time he has." She slipped Tooter another piece of bacon. "It could be months or even a year."

"Does it hurt him?"

Mom shook her head. "Dr. Ross says Tooter doesn't seem to be in any pain at all."

"But he's going to keep changing, isn't he?" I rubbed my cheek against his soft belly.

Mom sighed. "Yes."

I sat up and put my arms around Mom's neck. My mouth against her shoulder, I whispered, "You can't go back to being sad."

Slowly Mom's arms wrapped around me. "I'm not going anywhere."

Anthony Hamlin stopped by that night to tell us in person that Elizabeth McAllister was dropping all charges. I considered telling him it was because of me, not him, but he seemed way too proud of himself. I doubt he'd believe me anyway.

Chapter Seventeen

*R*emember *that Thursday* appointment? It was at Addison School for the Blind in Columbia.

"Most students only attend Addison School for a year or two," the director said, as Mom, Dad, and I sat in her crisp, white office. "We make sure our students not only are up to par academically with other students their age, but that they've mastered life skills. Everything from being able to navigate a new town to grocery shopping and ordering at a restaurant."

"And that's something students can pick up in a year?" asked Mom, leaning forward like a child about to receive a prize.

"Yes," the director answered. She had told me her name—Mrs. Something or Other—but it floated right out of my mind the moment she shared it. She had gray hair slicked back in a perfect bun and her desk was completely clear except for a vase filled with pink roses and a laptop. "We make sure that they do."

229

I stared out the window. This place, it was pretty amazing. Some of the students were totally blind *and* deaf. On the way in, I saw a couple kids with scars where their eyes should be. These kids, I could understand them needing a special school. But me? It made my stomach's insides feel slippery, like I was a fraud. I wasn't blind enough to need a special school. I mean, I could get around.

But here was Mom, with Dad nodding just beside her, shocked that I could learn to someday go to the grocery store by myself. Did that really surprise them? Why?

I squeezed my eyes shut and thought about it. Mom would drop me off at the store. No, scratch that. If I were independent, I'd have to find my own way. I squeezed my eyes tighter and erased the scene. This time, I walked up to the grocery store using my cane. I grabbed a cart. I shook my head, even though I knew I probably looked crazy to everyone else, and cleared the scene again. I couldn't take a cart if I had walked there. The most I'd be able to carry home would be what I could hold in a basket. So I pictured myself slipping the basket up my arm. Now, I needed some apples. I walked down the aisles, finding the apple row. I put a few in a bag and added it to my basket. Next, I wanted some hamburgers. I made my way to the meat department and stood in front of the packages of hamburger. I know Mom always checked the dates, which I guess were on the label. I imagined myself doing the same but soon had to clear the scene again. The print was too small. I couldn't make it out.

I pictured myself moving on to finding a certain spice—let's say cilantro—in the spice aisle. The spices were stacked on the highest shelf. I couldn't get close enough to read the labels.

Is this what it would be like? Or was I being too doom and gloom? How would this school help me get to where I needed to be? They wouldn't make labels bigger or shelves shorter. They wouldn't make me able to drive a car or see which apple was the freshest. It was pointless.

I folded over and rested my head against my knees while my parents and the director spoke. Like they suddenly remembered I existed—I was, after all, the entire reason we were there—the three of them turned to face me.

"Alice?" Dad asked. "What's wrong?"

"I don't belong here," I said under my breath, but they heard.

"What makes you say that?" Director Whatever-Her-Name-Is asked.

"I'm not *that* blind." I sat up straighter and glared at Mom and Dad. I was sure my nerves were making my eyes bob like crazy but my voice was steady. I didn't even realize it until then, but I had taken the gnome Mr. Hamlin had given me out of my pocket and was clutching it. The elf's pointy hat dug into my palm. "I can get around on my own already. I can read books—regular books. So what if I hold them closer? I don't want to go to this school."

Mom shifted in her seat and Dad started muttering things about me being rude.

"I'm sorry," I said to Director Whatever-Her-Name-Is. "Your school is beautiful. It's amazing, it really is. It's just not for me."

"Why don't you take a tour and then decide?" the director asked.

We started in the gardens. The school was in the middle of a park, with rose gardens and acres of vibrant green grass.

"What's the point?" I trailed behind Mom and Dad, taking sluggish steps around a koi pond. "It's not like the kids who go here can see the goldfish." They were huge goldfish but still only orange blurs in the dark water.

The tour guide stopped midsentence. Her unseeing eyes might not have focused on my face, but the way she clipped off her words left no doubt that she could go toe-to-toe with me on surliness. "The point is that beauty can be enjoyed by anyone willing to notice it. Yes, I might not see the fish. But I can feel the water with my fingers and toes. I can hear them gulp at food when I feed them. I can smell the musty, wet odor of the pond, the cold stone of the bridge. I can create the beauty with my mind. Can you?"

Mom's face flushed bright red. Dad grumbled something, but I didn't hear it. My mind was stuck on the tour guide's last phrase: "Create the beauty with my mind."

My feet moved a little faster.

When we got inside the sleek school, the tour guide—her name was Jessica (all the teachers went by their first name here)—called over a student. "Alice, I'd like you to meet Richie, a soon-to-be seventh grader."

Richie was about as tall as James with orange red hair and so many freckles even I could see them. His eyes were warm and brown. Richie smiled and held out his hand for me to shake. Let's just say Richie wasn't a big fan of personal space. He stood a couple inches too close to me, making me question suddenly if the onions on the turkey sandwich I had for lunch had been a good idea. "Name's Richie, but only teachers call me that. Everyone else calls me Ryder," he said. Ryder's eyes swept over me, head to toe.

Wait a second. His *eye* swept over me. The other eye? It didn't move.

Now, I've had plenty of experience with people staring weirdly at my eyes, so I tried not to do the same. Plus, Jessica introduced Ryder as a student. At a school for *the blind.* So of course something was wrong with his eyes. Or eye. Whatever. I wasn't going to stare.

"Ryder, why don't you show Alice around the computer lab while her family reviews some paperwork?" Jessica suggested.

"Sure." Ryder grabbed my wrist. "Follow me."

"I can follow on my own," I snapped.

"I know." But he didn't let go of my hand.

The lab was filled with computers screens as big as our television. Ryder showed me how they magnified books. I couldn't wipe away my smile when I realized I could sit back in my chair and still read the books. Seriously, sit *back.* "Pretty cool, huh?" Ryder said.

He showed me how I could listen to thousands of books, and I thought of how I could keep up with Kerica's book consumption. I learned about simpler things, too. Like a little stand I could put my books on that tilted the pages so they reflected less glare. I saw that none of the papers they used were white; they were all yellow or blue. "It helps curb visual fatigue," Ryder said.

"Is that something you have trouble with?" I hinted. I mean, among visual impairments, albinism isn't really fair. Everyone can tell. Other conditions, not so much.

"Nah," Ryder said with a smile that was infuriating. He totally knew I was digging.

"How long have you been here?" I asked after the tour.

"About a year. I'll go back to public in eighth grade."

"Is that normal? To go back to public?"

"Afraid you'll miss me?" Ryder cocked an eyebrow. "Don't worry. I'll be here for a year. I'll keep an eye out for you."

And to prove it, Ryder popped out his unmoving eye and held it in his palm.

I sucked in a gasp and squeezed my lips together to keep in a scream. I fought to make my face still even though I knew my eyes gave me up. Ryder casually put his artificial eye back in its socket.

"How long have you waited to use that line?" I asked, proud of my steady voice.

Ryder snorted. "Let's see, my eye was removed when I was seven so . . . six years?"

"It's a good joke. But it did make me feel a little ill. Do I look pale to you?" I held a white-as-paper hand in front of him.

"Maybe a little," he laughed.

A little later, Ryder had shown me just about the entire school minus the dormitories. Some kids boarded here, but many—like me—lived close enough to commute.

"Can I ask you something kind of personal?" I said.

Ryder stopped midstride and sighed dramatically. "This happens all the time. Women meet me, fall instantly in love. But no, I can't run away with you."

"And most of the girls you meet are blind . . ."

"What's your point, Porcelain?"

It was tough to keep my lips from twitching at that. "My *question*," I said, "is about your eye."

"This one?" Ryder pointed at his face. "Or this one?"

I grabbed his arm before he could pop the fake eye out again. "Stop!"

"Cancer, retinoblastoma. Basically tumors behind my eye."

I nodded. "Yeah, but you have your other eye. So you're not *blind* blind. What are you doing here?"

"You realize you just skipped over my whole cancer story, right? I mean, most people, they at least ask—"

"Sorry. But you're not *blind* blind, right?" I shuddered a little, thinking about how horrible I was being.

I hated, hated, hated when people questioned my blindness. Like because I could read or see when someone was in front of me I wasn't really blind. Yet here I was drilling this boy I just met about why he was at a school for the blind. But I had to know.

"My other eye had a couple tumors. The treatment brought my vision to 20/60. Not bad, right? But since it's my only eye, I wanted to make the most of it."

"You *wanted* to come here?" I asked.

"I want to make the most of what I have." Ryder crossed his arms. He stopped walking and stared at me straight on. "Let me ask you a personal question."

I nodded.

"Why *wouldn't* you want to go here?"

And you know what? I didn't have one good reason.

That week, instead of hanging out at the library, Kerica and I spent most of our time outside the diner as Kerica added her mural to the window. She was so thorough, adding the outline and making sure the brushes were straight before dipping them into paint. I could tell she was concentrating and so I tried to be quiet.

All I could think about was that everything was about to end. The Bartel School for Girls opened in three days. Addison School for the Blind began next week. We wouldn't have these long summer days anymore. It took me a long time to realize Kerica was looking at me instead of her artwork.

"Are you nervous?" she asked. I didn't know if she was asking about starting a new school or about the essay contest. Finalists were going to be notified that night. A nod applied to both so that's what I did.

"Don't be. You'll be fine. No matter what." She leaned in and carefully painted in the letters for the word WELCOME.

I sat down on the sidewalk to watch. Sandi tapped on the glass from the opposite side of the window and waved. She had come along to watch Kerica, too, but quickly ducked inside to sit next to Mayor Hank. She was hoping he'd slip and say if she was a finalist in the contest, I think.

Things with Sandi were a little odd. It's like she didn't know how not to be a jerk and I didn't know how to stay mad at her. Her mother had walked with her to the library the other day so she could check in with Mrs. Morris. Elizabeth McAllister had paused in front of where I was sitting. Her fists clenched and unclenched and I could feel her anger radiating off her just as clearly as I could feel love from my mom and dad when they were near me.

"Come on, Mom," Sandi had coaxed, but her mother stayed put in front of me.

I braced myself, but all she said was a super crisp, "Thank you for helping Sandi with her essay."

Surprised, my head jerked toward her. "You're welcome," I squeaked.

"I'm sure you'll be keeping her . . . condition . . . to yourself."

I nodded. For the first time in my life, I was glad I was blind so I didn't have to see Sandi's face.

Chapter Eighteen

Dear Miss Alice Confrey,
*We are pleased to inform you that your essay has been selected
as a finalist in the first annual Sinkville Success Stories competition. You and the other two candidates will have your essays
published on the town website and in the Sinkville Gazette. Residents will be able to vote on their favorite essay up until the day
before our reception, to which you and your family are cordially
invited. We will announce our winner at the reception.*

You should be pleased with your accomplishment.

Sincerely,

The Sinkville Success Stories Children's Contest Committee

Mom wore a blue dress that swung around her calves.
Dad didn't change out of the tie and white button-down
shirt that he wore to work. James slicked back the hair
that hung in his face for months, saw how white his
forehead underneath was compared to his tanned face,

and combed it back where it had been. But I appreciated the effort.

I smoothed my yellow sundress and tucked Tooter under my arm. He wouldn't be coming, of course, but I held him until the moment we left. We had been carrying him around since we had found out about his tumor. Sometimes he had trouble walking. But the real reason was we all just wanted to have him around all the time.

"Wish me luck today," I said, and Tooter licked my cheek.

The reception was held at the high school auditorium. And it was packed.

We had to read our essays on stage in front of everyone. My eyes fluttered so fast the edges of the room seemed to dance. The first person to go was the boy I had seen talking with Mayor Hank. His name was Josh Andros and I didn't hear a word of his essay. I was too busy concentrating on not peeing or pulling a Tooter on stage. I did hear the applause that drowned out my hammering heart. A couple of hoots, too.

Sandi was shaking just as hard as me as she went on stage. "You can do this," I whispered to her as she passed and she stopped and nodded to me. I knew she and Mrs. Morris had been practicing reading her essay all week. And she read it flawlessly.

"Wow," Josh said under his breath.

"What?" I whispered back as the crowd continued cheering. "I can't see."

Josh's face flushed but he answered, "The librarian and her daughter are giving a standing ovation."

I jumped out of my chair, too, and cheered.

Too soon, it was my turn. I swallowed a sour taste in my mouth as my name was called. My essay was in 36-point font, but I was so nervous I still had to hold it close to my face. At least, I did at first.

"The Sinkville Sycamore's roots run as deep as the town's history. It saw Native American camps. Revolutionary battles and civil war. It was there when countless couples fell in love picnicking in its shade. It held those couples' children in its limbs. It grew as our town grew. It never moved from Sinkville soil.

"Some storms scarred it. Some limbs were lost. Some people cut into its trunk. But the land supported it, allowing it to change and letting it grow. In the same way, the success of lifelong residents of Sinkville lies in their willingness to live simply, grow steadily, and weather their storms."

I took a deep breath and turned the page of my essay. The first part was about Mr. Hamlin, who was in the front row with Sarah. The crowd murmured when I spoke of the lake water flowing through his house and how he wished he had saved his mother's sink. There was a smattering of applause when I got to how Sarah would be going to college this year but plans to return to Sinkville.

I read what I had written about the Williams Diner welcoming everyone during the civil rights movement. How it's where Mill workers refresh before going home. My voice shook all over again when I spoke about how it's where a newcomer will realize she is at home.

A few people laughed when I talked about teenage Mayor Hank's awful handshake painting at Williams Diner, but more people said, "Hear, hear!" and whistled when I added that because of this town's support, they got the most passionate mayor possible. A few more cheered when I said an artist was bringing that handshake back to the diner's window.

I read about the unwanted frogs, turtles, and snakes finding a new home with Dr. Ross. I talked about how he worked to rehabilitate the animals others would give up on, like Chuck and the opossum babies.

My essay ended with more about the Sycamore. "When I sit under the Sinkville Sycamore, I cannot see the top of the tree. I see the limbs stretching toward the sky and know the roots dig just as deep. That is Sinkville's success."

No one clapped as I finished. No one.

I took an awkward step backward toward my chair, my face flaming so much that my eyes watered. Then an ear-splitting whistle cut the silence, followed with, "All right, Alice!" in my brother's voice.

And then the applause, breaking me apart and putting me back together.

Mom met me at the bottom of the stairs to lead me to our seats. Her face was wet as she pressed her cheek against mine. "I've never been more proud of my daughter," she whispered in my ear.

Gretel popped up from her seat to hug me as we walked by. I noticed Mayor Hank, seated next to her, take her hand when she sat back down.

Sarah stood by Mr. Hamlin's wheelchair at the end of our aisle. "I can't believe you're here!" I gushed and squeezed her grandfather's hand.

"Wouldn't miss it, Gnome Girl."

Anthony Hamlin shook my hand from his seat but kept his eyes on his dad. "I didn't know that story. I mean the whole story, about the lake," I heard him whisper.

"You did great." Sandi leaned forward from the row behind me and squeezed my shoulder when we finally reached our seats.

"You were amazing!" I whispered back, turning in my seat.

She put her mouth next to my ear so I could hear her whisper over the applause. "Mom said I could have anything I wanted if I could nail the essay speech. She's taking tomorrow off work. We're not shopping or anything. We're just going to hang out."

I grinned at Sandi and she smiled back.

Mayor Hank made his way to the stage, his hands raised to quiet the crowd. Just as they stopped clapping he said, "Let's give another hand to our young writers." And then the crowd erupted again.

All this applause and I'd soon be deaf as well as blind. But I smiled anyway.

I had done it. I made Sinkville my home. Next to me, Mom leaned forward to take a tissue from Mrs. Morris. Kerica was bouncing in her seat, just like Eliza used to do. Dad had his arm around James's shoulder. I squeezed my eyes to see it clearer and saw that we truly were like the Sycamore's roots, stretching out in hidden ways but staying connected.

I realized, it didn't matter who got the prize. I already won.

But I'm not going to lie: really winning was pretty awesome, too.

Acknowledgments

I had the privilege of growing up in a paper mill town like Sinkville and spent a lot of time catching fish and being chased by geese at a lake created to support the mill. The lake seemed so natural, making the glimpse of a driveway or road dipping into its depths fascinating.

My grandpa would tell me stories about a whole town under the water. As it turns out, the homes were razed before the water was pumped in, but I let Mr. Hamlin keep his drowned farmhouse intact.

Growing up, the mill smell never bothered me, but man! It hits me now when I come home to visit. What also hits me is the realization of how blessed I am to have such a charming hometown.

Family and friends who read Alice's story will certainly be able to pick out a few other inspired-by-true-events moments (seriously, do not provoke a squirrel). Despite the ties to real life, Alice's story is through and through her own. Much love and thanks go to those who gave me the time, encouragement, and insight to craft this tale.

Nicole Resciniti, super-agent and friend, thank you for believing in me and pushing me to dream bigger than I could've hoped. Thank you to my fantastic editor, Julie Matysik, whose love for these characters and their world means so much to me. Your talent brought this story to a whole new level.

Thank you, also, to the experts with Historic Columbia who shared their knowledge and time, which helped bring to life the fictional town of Sinkville. I am grateful for the insight from University of South Carolina History Professors Dr. Bobby Donaldson and Dr. Robert R. Weyeneth. Any errors with regards to accuracy are mine alone.

Much love also goes to the friends and family who read early versions of this story. Thank you, Buffy, for showing me that everybody has a story and for polishing this one. And to my cousin Dane, who not only responded but took seriously my hypothetical if-a-dog-pees-on-someone-can-that-person-sue question.

Mom, Dad, Amy, and Michele, thank you for cheering me on every step of this journey.

God blessed me with two amazing families, the one I was born into and the one I married into. Thank you, John, Debbi, Tim, and Amanda, for the love and encouragement.

I saved the best for last. Jon, I'll never be able to thank you enough for working so hard to create this beautiful life we share. Emma and Benny, you are endless sources of joy, love, and inspiration. But please, no more squirrels.

For more information about albinism and related visual impairments, please check out NOAH (National Organization for Albinism and Hypopigmentation) at www.albinism.org.

For more about the civil rights movement in South Carolina, check out Historic Columbia at www.historic-columbia.org.

About the Author

*B*eth *Vrabel grew* up in a small paper mill town in Pennsylvania. She won a short-story contest in fourth grade and promptly decided writing was what she was going to do with her life. Although her other plans—becoming a wolf biologist, a Yellowstone National Park ranger, and a professional roller skater—didn't come to fruition, she stuck with the writing. A graduate of Pennsylvania State University, Beth was a features columnist and editor before becoming an author. Beth also writes the *Pack of Dorks* series.

Keep your eyes peeled
for...

pack of dorks
CAMP DORK

BETH VRABEL

available from
Sky Pony Press
May 2016!